Sammy's Monsters and the Magic of Roman & Jude

Sammy's Monster Adventures, Volume 4

Freya Jobe

Published by Freya Jobe, 2024.

This is a work of fiction. Similarities to real people, places, or events are entirely coincidental.

SAMMY'S MONSTERS AND THE MAGIC OF ROMAN & JUDE

First edition. November 3, 2024.

Copyright © 2024 Freya Jobe.

ISBN: 979-8227756954

Written by Freya Jobe.

Sammy's Monsters and the Magic of Roman & Jude

Years ago, Sammy's life was filled with magic, laughter, and a group of lovable, silly monsters who transformed his world. They were Whiffle, the sparkly mischief-maker; Blinky, the gentle glow that lit the way; Munch, the snack-loving friend with a heart as big as his appetite; and Mumbles, the quiet, mysterious one whose whispers carried wisdom. Together, they brought Sammy unforgettable adventures, magical mischief, and a friendship that he'd carry in his heart forever.

Now, Sammy is all grown up, and he has a family of his own. His two children, Roman and Jude, have grown up hearing bedtime stories about their dad's magical monster friends. Tales of glittery dances, glowing light shows, and snack-filled feasts have kept the monsters alive in their imaginations. Every night, they beg Sammy to tell them more, secretly hoping that one day, they'll meet the magical creatures he calls his best friends.

One summer night, as Roman and Jude drift off to sleep, they spot something unusual—a faint glow under their bed, a trail of glitter leading down the hall, and a few cookie crumbs left behind. Could it be? The monsters are back!

This is the story of Roman and Jude's own magical monster adventures, as they discover their dad's old friends and forge their own bond with the creatures who brought him so much joy. With Whiffle's glittery surprises, Blinky's glowing light, Munch's endless snacks, and Mumbles' quiet magic, they're in for a summer of laughter, discovery, and memories that will last a lifetime.

Because sometimes, the best friends you'll ever make are the ones who are just a little bit magical—and a whole lot silly.

Chapter 1: A Story Before Bedtime

Sammy settled down on the edge of Roman and Jude's bed, glancing fondly at his two sons. They were nestled under a blanket, eyes wide with curiosity as they anticipated their dad's latest story. It had become a cherished bedtime tradition—each night, Sammy would share tales from his own college days, but not the ordinary kind. No, his stories were a little different, filled with magic, mystery, and, of course, monsters.

Sammy's boys had grown up on these stories, hanging on to every word. They adored hearing about his silly, lovable monster friends, though they had never seen one for themselves. Still, the stories made them feel like they had—a different monster for every personality, each with a unique kind of magic that seemed almost real.

"Are you going to tell us about the monsters again, Dad?" Roman asked, tugging the blanket up to his chin.

Sammy chuckled. "You know, I don't think I can ever top the stories I've already told you. But... maybe I could start from the beginning tonight?"

Jude's face lit up. "Yes! Start from the very first time you met them!"

"Alright," Sammy said, settling in. "But remember, this story goes way back to when I was just a college student, new to campus. I had no idea what was in store for me. I didn't know that my life was about to get... magical."

He paused for a moment, letting the excitement build. Roman and Jude sat completely still, their eyes glued to their dad as he started to tell his story.

"I was having a tough time settling in at first," Sammy began, looking thoughtful. "College was bigger and busier than anything I'd known. The classes, the new faces, the huge campus... it was overwhelming. But one night, something happened that changed everything."

The boys leaned closer, hanging on to every word.

"I was lying in bed, just like you are now," Sammy continued, "when I saw something strange. It was a faint glow in the corner of my room. At first, I thought I was imagining it, but the light got brighter and brighter until I couldn't ignore it anymore."

Jude's eyes widened. "Was it Blinky?"

Sammy grinned. "You got it. I didn't know it was him back then, though. I just saw this soft, warm light moving around the room. I thought maybe someone had left a flashlight on or something. So, I got up to investigate. But when I looked closer, I realized this light wasn't just moving by itself—it was floating in the air."

Roman gasped. "What did you do?"

"Well," Sammy said, raising his eyebrows, "I didn't really know what to do. I watched the light for a while, feeling like I'd stumbled into a dream. And then I heard a voice, soft and gentle, like a whisper in the breeze. 'Hello,' it said, and I jumped about three feet into the air. That was the moment I met Blinky."

The boys giggled, imagining their dad being surprised by a floating light.

"Blinky's glow was like nothing I'd ever seen before. It wasn't just light—it felt like it carried warmth, kindness, and a bit of magic. He explained that he was here to help me settle in, to make my college days a little brighter."

"What happened next?" Jude whispered, his face filled with awe.

"Not long after, I met the rest of the gang," Sammy said, smiling at the memory. "One day, I found glitter everywhere in my room, and I couldn't figure out where it was coming from. Then I heard a tiny giggle, like a little bell ringing, and suddenly, there was a burst of sparkles right in front of me. That's when Whiffle appeared."

"Whiffle!" Roman exclaimed. "The glitter monster!"

"Exactly," Sammy said, chuckling. "Whiffle loved causing little sparkly mischief. He thought life was better with a bit of glitter and never missed a chance to toss some around. I couldn't be upset, though—his laughter was contagious, and he always knew how to make me smile. Wherever he went, a trail of sparkles followed, and life just seemed... brighter."

"Blinky and Whiffle became my first monster friends," Sammy continued. "But things didn't stop there. One night, I came back to my dorm and found half my snacks missing. I searched the room, but the only sign of the culprit was a little pile of crumbs leading to a closet. And guess who was hiding there?"

"Munch!" Jude said, his face lighting up.

Sammy nodded. "Yes, Munch. A big-hearted monster with an even bigger appetite! He apologized for eating my snacks but admitted he couldn't help it. Snacks were his favorite thing in the world, and he promised to share next time. From that day on, he'd sneak in to share his latest snack creations with me, even teaching me a few of his monster-approved recipes. His passion for food was infectious."

Roman and Jude giggled, picturing Munch sneaking into their dad's room, munching on cookies and crackers.

"But Munch wasn't the only one hiding surprises," Sammy continued. "There was also Mumbles. Mumbles didn't show himself right away. He was... quieter than the others, a bit more mysterious. I'd hear faint whispers or feel a soft breeze at night, but I couldn't see him. It took a while, but one night, I caught sight of him—a soft, misty figure in the moonlight, floating near the window."

"What was Mumbles like?" Roman asked, intrigued.

Sammy smiled, thinking of his gentle, quiet friend. "Mumbles was wise and calming. He didn't say much, but he always seemed to know when I needed a reassuring word or a little advice. He could disappear into thin air, and his voice was like a soft breeze. He made me feel safe, like I was never truly alone."

The boys were silent, hanging on every word. Sammy paused, letting the memories wash over him. It felt like just yesterday that he'd been with them, sharing laughs, adventures, and secrets. His monster friends had turned his college days into something magical, something unforgettable.

"Over the years, we had all sorts of adventures together," Sammy continued, his voice soft and nostalgic. "They were always by my side, through every challenge, every tough night, and every celebration. I can't tell you how much they changed my life. They taught me about friendship, laughter, and seeing the world through a magical lens. I don't know if I would've made it through college without them."

Roman and Jude looked at him with wide, amazed eyes. "Dad, do you think they're... still around?" Jude asked quietly, hope gleaming in his eyes.

Sammy smiled, a glimmer of mischief in his eyes. "Well, they are magical, you know. And magic like that doesn't just disappear. But the thing about monster friends is... they tend to show up when you least expect it. And who knows? Maybe if you're really lucky, you might catch a glimpse of them yourselves someday."

The boys exchanged a hopeful glance, their imaginations racing with thoughts of glitter trails, glowing lights, and friendly monsters hiding in the corners of their own room.

As Sammy tucked them in, Roman and Jude could hardly contain their excitement. "Dad, will you tell us more tomorrow night?" Roman asked, his voice full of anticipation.

"Of course," Sammy said, smiling warmly. "I have so many stories left to share. But remember, magic only happens when you believe in it. So keep your eyes open and your hearts ready. You never know when a bit of monster magic might find its way into your life."

He kissed them goodnight and turned off the light, leaving the room in a comfortable, quiet darkness. But just as he closed the door, he could've sworn he saw a faint shimmer of glitter in the corner, catching the moonlight.

Sammy's heart filled with warmth as he smiled to himself. Maybe, just maybe, the monsters were already closer than his boys realized.

Chapter 2: The Mysterious Sparkles

Roman squinted as a glimmer caught his eye, a tiny sparkle shining just below the hallway light. He and Jude had just woken up, eager to start the day, but this glittery trail had stopped them in their tracks. The boys exchanged curious glances and knelt down for a closer look.

A faint line of glitter trailed along the floor, shimmering faintly and leading... somewhere. It was as if someone—or something—had left a sparkly path, waiting for them to follow.

"Roman," Jude whispered, pointing at the tiny sparkles that glistened like stardust. "Do you think this could be...?"

Roman's face lit up, remembering their dad's bedtime story from the night before. "You're thinking what I'm thinking," he replied, a grin spreading across his face. "Let's follow it."

They padded quietly down the hall, not wanting to lose sight of the trail. The glitter sparkled faintly in the early morning light, guiding them around corners, through doorways, and finally... straight to the living room.

The boys stopped just outside the door. The glittery path curved around the room, looping around furniture, swirling over the carpet, and even sprinkling along the bookshelves, leaving a glistening pattern as if a tiny, invisible creature had danced its way through.

Jude's eyes grew wide. "This is exactly what Dad said it would look like."

Roman nodded, his heart racing with excitement. "It has to be... it just has to."

They moved forward, stepping carefully around the glittery path, afraid to disturb even a single speck. But as they made their way across the room, they heard the faintest sound—a soft giggle, like tiny bells ringing in the air. Roman and Jude froze, glancing around the room, but nothing was there. The only sound was that faint, cheerful giggle, echoing as if it was coming from nowhere and everywhere at once.

Jude's face lit up, and he grabbed his brother's arm. "Did you hear that?"

Roman nodded, his eyes darting around, trying to catch any sign of movement. "Maybe... maybe we should check over by the bookshelf," he suggested, pointing to where the glitter trail ended in a small, sparkly pile.

They tiptoed over, each of them holding their breath. The closer they got, the brighter the pile of glitter seemed to shine. And then, just as they were about to reach the end of the trail, the giggle came again—only louder this time, filling the room with cheerful, mischievous energy.

The boys spun around, wide-eyed, searching the room. But whatever had left that glitter trail was nowhere to be seen.

They exchanged glances, both of them bursting with excitement and wonder. "Do you think... it was Whiffle?" Jude asked, his voice barely more than a whisper.

Roman grinned, his eyes sparkling as brightly as the glitter. "I think it was. And I think we're going to have more to find soon."

As they glanced back at the glittery trail, they couldn't help but feel as if they'd stepped into one of their dad's magical stories.

Chapter 3: Meet Whiffle, the Glitter Monster

It was early the next morning when Roman and Jude woke up to find more glitter trails crisscrossing the hallway. The boys were beyond curious now. This was the second day in a row they'd seen sparkles appearing mysteriously around the house, and they were certain something magical was going on.

"Do you think we'll find him today?" Jude whispered, excitement buzzing in his voice.

Roman nodded, grinning. "We have to."

They followed the glitter trail carefully, noticing that it seemed to shimmer more brightly today, almost as if it were glowing just for them. The trail led them down the hallway, into the living room, and finally, around the corner toward the playroom. As they reached the door, they heard a faint giggle—a familiar, cheerful sound, like the one they'd heard the day before.

The boys exchanged excited glances and tiptoed inside. There, perched on the arm of the couch, was the tiniest, sparkiest creature they had ever seen. He was covered from head to toe in glitter, which seemed to swirl around him like a magical dust storm. His bright, twinkling eyes sparkled with excitement, and his wide smile made him look both friendly and full of mischief.

"Hello there!" he said, his voice a soft, cheerful jingle. "I've been waiting for you two."

Roman and Jude were momentarily speechless, their eyes wide with wonder.

"Are... are you Whiffle?" Roman finally managed to ask.

Whiffle grinned even wider, his whole body lighting up with excitement. "The one and only! And you must be Roman and Jude, Sammy's boys."

The boys beamed, nodding enthusiastically.

"Your dad told me so much about you," Whiffle said, his voice filled with joy. "I couldn't resist coming by to say hello. We had so many adventures together, your dad and I. And I thought it was about time I found some new adventurers to join me!"

Roman and Jude's faces lit up, their hearts racing with excitement. "What kind of adventures?" Jude asked, hardly able to contain himself.

"Oh, all sorts of adventures!" Whiffle replied, his eyes twinkling with excitement. "Glittery ones, of course. Your dad and I used to have epic glitter battles—he'd try to dodge them, but I always got him in the end. We even filled an entire dorm room with sparkles once, and he was still finding glitter in his socks months later!"

Roman and Jude burst out laughing, imagining their dad trying to dodge clouds of glitter and failing miserably.

"But that wasn't all," Whiffle continued, leaning in as if sharing a big secret. "We'd have nighttime dance parties, hide-and-seek games, and scavenger hunts where the prize was something silly, like a cookie crumb I'd hidden ages ago. Your dad loved every bit of it, though he'd never admit how much."

Jude's eyes were shining. "And... do you think... maybe we could join in on an adventure too?"

Whiffle's face lit up. "I was hoping you'd ask! Adventures are always better with friends."

The boys grinned, feeling like the luckiest kids in the world. Here they were, talking to a real, live glitter monster—one who'd been their dad's friend for years and who was now inviting them to join in the fun.

"Come on," Whiffle said, jumping off the couch with a sprinkle of sparkles. "Let's start with a little tour. I've hidden something special around here, just for you two. If you can find it, maybe it'll lead to an even bigger adventure!"

Roman and Jude's faces lit up, and they eagerly followed Whiffle as he led them around the playroom, glitter trailing behind him like a sparkling map. Their magical adventure had only just begun, and already, they knew this was going to be a summer they'd never forget.

Chapter 4: A Glowing Surprise

That night, after an exciting day spent with Whiffle, Roman and Jude could hardly sleep. The memory of the glittery, mischievous monster danced in their minds, filling them with excitement. They wondered about the other magical creatures their dad had mentioned—could they really be just as real as Whiffle?

As the house grew quiet, a soft glow began to fill their room, casting a gentle, warm light across the walls. Roman blinked, noticing the change, and nudged his brother.

"Jude, look," he whispered, pointing to the strange glow. "Something's... glowing."

The boys sat up, eyes wide, as they noticed a soft light floating near the end of their bed. The glow was warm, like candlelight, but with a steady, calm rhythm that seemed to pulse gently, as if it had a heartbeat. The boys stared, mesmerized, until the light began to shift and form into a shape—a small, round figure with two friendly eyes that looked directly at them.

"Good evening, Roman and Jude," said a soft, comforting voice. The creature's glow pulsed slightly, brightening with each word. "I'm Blinky."

The boys couldn't hide their amazement. "Blinky!" Roman gasped, remembering their dad's stories. "You're really here!"

Blinky's glow shimmered a little brighter. "I wouldn't miss the chance to meet Sammy's boys. Your dad was one of my very first friends, and he told me all about you two. I thought it was time I came by to say hello."

Jude, still wide-eyed, leaned a little closer. "Are you really... made of light?"

Blinky chuckled, his glow flickering gently. "In a way, yes. My glow is my special power. It's how I can light up dark places, show the way, or even help people feel calm when they're scared."

The boys exchanged awed glances. They had never seen anything like this before. Blinky wasn't like a flashlight or a nightlight; his glow was different, warmer, like a hug wrapped in light.

"Your glow is so... peaceful," Jude whispered, reaching out a hand toward Blinky's gentle light. "Does it hurt you to glow like that?"

Blinky chuckled softly, floating closer so they could see the delicate layers of his warm light. "Not at all! In fact, glowing is what I'm best at. It's my way of being there for my friends, to brighten their path or make them feel safe."

Roman tilted his head, his curiosity growing. "Dad said you helped him through tough nights when he felt alone. Is that true?"

Blinky nodded, his eyes kind. "That's right. Your dad had some nights when things felt a little overwhelming, and I'd sit by his bed and light up his room until he felt calm again. That's what friends are for, right?"

The boys nodded, feeling a newfound respect for Blinky and the special gift he shared. It was clear that Blinky's glow was more than just light—it was a gift of comfort and reassurance, something magical and kind.

"Would you like to see something special?" Blinky asked, his glow brightening.

Roman and Jude nodded eagerly.

"Alright," Blinky said, hovering near the middle of the room. "Close your eyes for a moment, and then open them when I say so."

The boys squeezed their eyes shut, buzzing with anticipation. They waited, feeling Blinky's glow warm the room around them.

"Now... open!" Blinky's voice was filled with excitement.

Roman and Jude opened their eyes, and what they saw left them speechless. Blinky had cast hundreds of tiny lights across the ceiling and walls, making their room look like a sparkling night sky. The lights twinkled softly, pulsing with Blinky's steady glow, creating a scene that looked like it had been plucked right out of a dream.

"It's like... a whole galaxy!" Roman whispered, his eyes wide with wonder.

Blinky's light grew warmer. "This is one of my favorite tricks. I wanted to give you a little piece of the night sky to help you feel calm and safe whenever you need it."

Jude reached out, as if trying to touch the stars on the ceiling. "It's beautiful, Blinky. I feel like I could reach up and grab one of those stars."

Blinky chuckled, hovering close by. "I think you two are going to make wonderful friends. And whenever you need a little light—whether it's for an adventure, or just to brighten up your room—I'll be here."

The boys sat quietly, soaking in the peaceful glow. The soft, steady light reminded them of the magical adventures their dad had described, of the laughter, the quiet nights, and the friendship that had grown between him and his magical monster friends.

Roman looked over at Blinky, his face thoughtful. "Dad always said magic was about more than what you could see. He said it was about feeling it, too. I think I finally get what he meant."

Blinky's glow flickered warmly, like a proud smile. "Your dad was right. Magic isn't just glitter and glow. It's about what it brings out in you—the kindness, the bravery, the curiosity. You two have it in you, just like your dad."

Jude and Roman beamed, feeling something warm and hopeful stir in their hearts.

The three of them sat quietly, gazing up at the glittering sky Blinky had cast across the room, feeling the magic of friendship fill the space around them. For a while, they were perfectly still, just taking in the moment.

As the boys began to drift off to sleep, Blinky hovered near their beds, his soft glow casting a comforting light over them.

"Goodnight, Roman and Jude," Blinky whispered, his light dimming to a gentle pulse. "I'll be here, watching over you."

With Blinky's glow lighting up their dreams, Roman and Jude slipped into sleep, feeling safer and more excited than ever for what other surprises and new friendships might await them.

Chapter 5: The Cookie Monster (Not That One!)

It was the weekend, and Roman and Jude were already buzzing with excitement. In just a few days, they'd met not one, but two of their dad's magical monster friends, Whiffle and Blinky. Whiffle's glittery mischief and Blinky's warm, calming glow had made them eager to see if any more of their dad's monster friends might pay them a visit.

"Do you think there are more?" Jude asked, peeking around every corner in the house, half-expecting another magical creature to pop up.

"Dad said he had a few monster friends," Roman replied, thinking back to the stories. "Maybe... if we keep our eyes open, we'll meet them."

Just as they walked into the kitchen, a strange noise caught their attention. It was a soft crunch, crunch, crunch, followed by a happy hum. The boys froze, exchanging a glance filled with excitement and curiosity.

"Did you hear that?" Roman whispered, his eyes wide.

Jude nodded, his own face lighting up with anticipation. They took a few quiet steps forward, peeking around the kitchen island, and there, sitting by the cookie jar, was a plump, cheerful monster with big, round eyes and a crumb-covered smile.

The monster was completely absorbed in his snack, happily munching on a cookie. He had soft, doughy fur, round cheeks, and wore a scarf that looked suspiciously like it was covered in crumbs. As the boys took in his appearance, the monster looked up, startled, and froze with a cookie halfway to his mouth.

"Oh!" he exclaimed, quickly brushing cookie crumbs from his face. "Hello there! I didn't think I'd be meeting anyone quite so soon."

Roman's eyes sparkled with recognition. "Are you... Munch?"

SAMMY'S MONSTERS AND THE MAGIC OF ROMAN & JUDE

The monster's face broke into a delighted grin. "The one and only! And you two must be Roman and Jude, Sammy's boys!"

The boys beamed. They were thrilled to meet another one of their dad's friends, and judging by the crumbs scattered around Munch, they already had a sense of what made him special.

"Dad said you love snacks," Jude said, eyeing the half-empty cookie jar.

"Oh, I do!" Munch replied, his eyes twinkling with excitement. "In fact, snacks are my specialty. I like to think of myself as a 'Snack Connoisseur.' I know the best ways to enjoy every kind of treat!"

Roman's face lit up. "Could you show us?"

Munch chuckled, patting the cookie jar. "I'd be delighted! How about we have a proper 'monster-approved' snack break? But first, let me make sure we're all stocked up. There's nothing worse than running low on snacks, you know."

He pulled out his own little snack pouch, which seemed to be filled with an endless assortment of treats—cookies, crackers, small bags of popcorn, even little jars of peanut butter. Roman and Jude's eyes grew wide as they watched Munch unpack his treasures, lining up a snack buffet right on the kitchen counter.

"Alright!" Munch said with a satisfied grin. "Now, the key to a good snack break is variety. You have to have a little of everything, or you'll get bored! And remember, the more flavours, the better."

He handed Roman and Jude each a cookie, then added a handful of popcorn and a few crackers to their plates. "Try a bite of each, one after the other," he instructed. "You'll see—it makes each taste even better."

The boys followed his advice, taking turns sampling each snack. Munch was right—the mix of flavours made the whole snack break feel like an adventure in itself.

"This is amazing!" Jude said, his mouth full of cookie and popcorn. "I've never tasted snacks like this before!"

Munch's eyes twinkled with pride. "Well, that's the magic of monster snacking! And remember, a true snack break is as much about sharing as it is about the food. It's always better when you've got friends to snack with."

Roman grinned, thinking of all the stories their dad had shared about Munch's endless appetite and his knack for finding snacks in unexpected places. "Did you and our dad used to have snack breaks like this?"

"Oh, absolutely!" Munch replied, nodding eagerly. "Your dad and I would have snack breaks at least once a day. He'd bring his snacks, I'd bring mine, and we'd see who had the best. We even had snack battles sometimes—who could make the crunchiest, chewiest, or most delicious snack!"

The boys laughed, picturing their dad in a snack-eating showdown with Munch. They were pretty sure Munch would have been the winner, given his clear expertise.

As they chatted, Munch shared more stories of his time with their dad. He told them about the late-night snack missions they'd go on, sneaking into the dorm kitchen to "borrow" a few extra treats, and the "Snack of the Week" competitions, where they'd try out new recipes each week to see who could come up with the best one.

"One time," Munch said, chuckling, "I made a popcorn tower as tall as your dad! We stacked every kernel until it reached the ceiling. Of course, it only lasted a few minutes before we ate the whole thing, but it was quite a sight!"

Roman and Jude could hardly contain their laughter. They imagined the popcorn tower and the look on their dad's face when it was finally ready. Munch's stories made the idea of "snack breaks" seem like a true adventure.

As their plates started to empty, Munch reached into his pouch again and pulled out a small tin labelled "Monster Munch Mix." He opened it and handed each of them a handful. The mix was filled with things they'd never tried before—mini marshmallows, tiny chocolate-covered pretzels, and what looked like rainbow-colored sprinkles.

"This, my friends, is the ultimate monster snack," Munch said proudly. "A little bit of sweet, a little bit of salty, and a whole lot of fun!"

The boys tried a bite, and their eyes widened in delight. The mix was everything Munch promised and more.

"This is the best snack I've ever had!" Jude exclaimed, savouring each bite.

Munch beamed, his round cheeks crinkling with pride. "That's the power of a monster-approved snack break. Food tastes even better when you're enjoying it with friends."

Just as they finished their last handfuls, Munch looked at them with a playful gleam in his eye. "How about a snack mission next time? I'll hide a treat somewhere, and you two have to find it. Sound like a challenge?"

Roman and Jude grinned, eager for the next adventure. "We're ready!"

With a full belly and a happy heart, Munch waved goodbye, leaving a small pile of crumbs as a reminder of their delicious snack break.

As Roman and Jude watched him disappear, they felt a warmth spread through them. They'd just experienced their first true monster-approved snack break, and they knew it wouldn't be their last.

Chapter 6: Secrets in the Attic

The morning was bright and peaceful, but Roman and Jude were already bursting with excitement after the past few days. Meeting Whiffle, Blinky, and Munch had been an adventure beyond their wildest dreams. Every night, they drifted off to sleep wondering if another magical creature might appear, and every morning, they woke up with new questions about their dad's college days with his monster friends.

As they finished breakfast, a familiar, cheerful giggle floated through the hallway. Roman and Jude perked up, recognizing the sound immediately.

"It's Whiffle!" Jude whispered excitedly.

They dashed toward the sound and found Whiffle hovering at the base of the attic stairs, his glittery form practically vibrating with excitement.

"Good morning, boys!" Whiffle greeted them with a playful twinkle in his eye. "I was just thinking, since you've already met some of my friends, it's time you saw something special."

Roman and Jude exchanged curious glances. "What is it?" Roman asked, practically bouncing with excitement.

Whiffle winked. "Come with me to the attic, and you'll see."

The boys followed Whiffle up the creaky wooden stairs to the attic, a place they'd rarely visited before. Sunlight filtered in through a small window, casting a warm glow over the dusty, quiet space. Boxes and old furniture were scattered around, each item telling a story from the past.

Whiffle floated ahead, weaving between stacks of boxes, leaving a shimmering trail of glitter in his wake. He came to a stop in front of a large, old trunk tucked in the corner. The trunk was covered in a fine layer of dust, and Roman noticed that it was marked with a faint sticker that read Property of Sammy.

"This," Whiffle said with a grin, "is your dad's college trunk. It's filled with keepsakes from his time with us."

Roman's and Jude's eyes widened with excitement. Their dad had kept a box of memories from his monster-filled days? They couldn't believe it!

"Can... can we open it?" Jude asked, barely containing his enthusiasm.

Whiffle nodded, his own eyes twinkling. "Of course! It's high time these memories got to see the light of day again."

The boys carefully lifted the lid of the trunk, revealing a treasure trove of items that looked like they'd been untouched for years. Right on top, they found an old, faded picture of their dad standing in what looked like a college dorm room, surrounded by what seemed to be shimmering, glittery spots. Roman held up the photo, his eyes wide.

"Is that... you, Whiffle?" he asked, pointing to one of the faint sparkles in the background.

Whiffle chuckled, peering over Roman's shoulder. "It sure is! Your dad was always trying to catch me off guard with his camera, but I was a little too quick. I'm afraid I mostly showed up as sparkles."

Roman and Jude laughed, imagining their dad trying to capture Whiffle's quick, glittery movements on film.

They dug further into the trunk, discovering old notebooks filled with doodles and scribbled notes about different "adventures" Sammy had shared with his monster friends. Roman picked up one of the notebooks, flipping through the pages. He noticed entries titled "The Great Glitter Battle" and "Monster Midnight Snack Raid," each one written in their dad's neat handwriting.

"Your dad used to document all our adventures," Whiffle explained with a fond smile. "He always wanted to remember every moment. And, well, let's just say there were plenty of memorable ones."

Jude pulled out a small, sparkly vial from the trunk, filled with what looked like tiny flecks of silver and gold. He held it up to the light, watching as the glitter swirled inside.

"What's this?" he asked, mesmerized.

Whiffle's eyes sparkled. "Ah, that's my 'emergency glitter.' I gave it to your dad one day after he told me he might miss me when I wasn't around. I figured, if he ever needed a reminder of me, he could just sprinkle a bit of glitter and feel like I was there with him."

Roman and Jude looked at each other, touched by the gesture. They were beginning to realize just how close their dad had been with his monster friends.

Next, Roman found a small jar labelled "Blinky's Glow Stones." Inside were tiny, faintly glowing stones in different colors, like pieces of a broken rainbow.

"Blinky gave these to your dad after his first final exams," Whiffle explained. "He wanted to make sure Sammy always had a bit of light during tough times. Each glow stone was meant to remind him to keep shining, even when things were hard."

Jude carefully put the jar back, feeling a sense of awe for the monsters' friendship with their dad. They were learning so much about him through these keepsakes—each item held a story, a piece of his past that made him who he was.

Suddenly, they heard a soft rustling sound and glanced down to see a small stack of postcards. Each one was covered in tiny drawings and colorful doodles. Roman picked one up and read aloud:

"'Dear Sammy, hope you're not running out of snacks. Here's a list of new recipes to try. Love, Munch.'"

The boys giggled, imagining Munch sending their dad snack recipes in the mail. Jude held up another postcard, which was decorated with sparkles and doodles of stars and planets.

"Look, this one's from Blinky!" Jude said, beaming. "It says, 'Remember, you're never alone in the dark.'"

Whiffle watched the boys as they carefully examined each keepsake, feeling a mixture of pride and nostalgia. "Your dad kept these because we had a friendship that was one of a kind," he said softly. "And I think, in his heart, he knew you two would love to know about it someday."

Roman and Jude exchanged a look, feeling a deeper understanding of their dad and his bond with his magical friends. They couldn't wait to hear more stories and make memories of their own.

Just as they were about to close the trunk, Jude noticed one last item—a small, leather-bound journal. It had Sammy's name on the cover, and when they opened it, they found sketches of each monster, drawn with remarkable detail. Each page was filled with descriptions, funny anecdotes, and little reminders about his monster friends.

"Look, it's a whole section just for Whiffle!" Roman said, pointing to a page filled with sparkly doodles and a note that read, "Always brings a smile, even on the worst days."

Jude flipped to the next page, where their dad had drawn Blinky's soft glow and had written, "My light when things seem dark."

Munch's page was next, covered in doodles of cookies, crackers, and sandwiches, with the note, "A friend for every snack break."

And finally, they found Mumbles' page, decorated with soft, swirling lines, reading, "A gentle voice to guide me, even when he's invisible."

As they closed the journal, Roman and Jude felt like they'd discovered a hidden part of their dad, one that only his monster friends truly knew. They looked up at Whiffle, their eyes filled with gratitude.

"Thank you for showing us this," Roman said quietly. "It's like we're getting to know Dad all over again."

Whiffle smiled, his face lighting up with pride. "You're very welcome, boys. And who knows? Maybe someday, you'll add a few keepsakes of your own to this box."

The boys grinned, their hearts filled with excitement for the adventures yet to come. With one last look at the treasures in the trunk, they closed the lid, knowing they'd just uncovered a magical piece of their family's past.

Chapter 7: Learning Monster-ese

Roman and Jude had spent every spare moment thinking about the magical items they'd found in the attic. Each one had told a story, showing them how close their dad had been to his monster friends. They couldn't wait to learn even more and make memories of their own. But out of all their dad's friends, there was still one they hadn't met—Mumbles.

As they finished breakfast one morning, a gentle breeze blew through the kitchen, carrying with it a faint, whispery hum. Roman and Jude glanced at each other, their eyes lighting up.

"Do you think…?" Jude whispered.

Just then, a soft, swirling mist appeared in the doorway, taking shape bit by bit until a faint, ghostly figure floated in front of them. The figure had soft, rounded edges, like the gentlest cloud, and large, kind eyes that seemed to sparkle with wisdom and warmth.

"Hello, boys," came a quiet, soothing voice that seemed to fill the room like a gentle breeze. "I'm Mumbles."

Roman and Jude grinned with excitement. Finally, they were meeting Mumbles, the last of their dad's magical friends.

"It's so nice to meet you!" Roman said eagerly. "We've been hoping you'd come!"

Mumbles gave a soft chuckle, his misty form swirling slightly. "I've been looking forward to it too. I heard you've already met Whiffle, Blinky, and Munch?"

The boys nodded. "They've been amazing," Jude said, beaming. "And they've told us all kinds of stories about you."

Mumbles' eyes twinkled. "Well, I have a few stories of my own. But before we get into that, how about a little lesson? I thought you might like to learn a bit of 'monster-ese,' our language."

Roman and Jude's faces lit up. Learning a monster language sounded incredible!

"Yes, please!" they said in unison.

Mumbles floated a little closer, his voice lowering to a whisper. "Monster-ese is a very special language," he began. "It's mostly spoken in whispers and soft sounds. You see, our words are often more like feelings, and sometimes... they can be a bit tricky for humans."

Roman nodded thoughtfully. "But we're ready! We can handle it!"

Jude nodded in agreement. "Yeah! Teach us something!"

Mumbles tilted his head, thinking for a moment. "Alright, let's start with something simple. One of the most common phrases we use is 'Fogglum frissle.' It's a general greeting and can mean anything from 'hello' to 'goodbye,' depending on how you say it."

The boys repeated the phrase, stumbling a little over the strange sounds. "Fuh... fogliss frangle?"

Mumbles chuckled. "Close! Try it a bit softer: Fogglum frissle."

They tried again, whispering it this time. "Fogglum frissle."

Mumbles nodded approvingly. "Excellent! Now, let's move on to something fun. 'Shimmer-tiddly-tum' means 'let's have fun.' Whiffle used it all the time with your dad. It's like saying, 'let's be silly!'"

"Shimmer-tiddly-tum!" Jude said, giggling as he tried to get his mouth around the funny sounds.

Roman laughed, "Shimmer-tidly-bum!" He clapped his hands to his mouth, realizing he'd mixed up the word.

Mumbles' eyes crinkled with amusement. "It's okay; Monster-ese can be tricky! But remember, it's about feeling, too. So say it with some excitement!"

The boys tried again, this time with big smiles, and each gave a cheerful "Shimmer-tiddly-tum!" that left them both laughing.

"Alright," Mumbles said, swirling around them. "Now, here's a phrase you might find useful. 'Snorffle-wozz.' It means 'I don't understand.' If you're ever confused, this one can help."

Roman repeated it carefully, "Snorffle-wozz."

Jude joined in, "Snorffle... wazz?"

Mumbles shook his head with a chuckle. "It's close, but make sure to say the 'wozz' part nice and soft—wozz, like a quiet breeze."

They gave it a few more tries, each version coming out a little funnier than the last. By the end, they had created their own interpretations that made Mumbles laugh along with them.

"Alright," Mumbles said, smiling. "How about one more? This one's a bit tricky. 'Trumble-grom' means 'thank you.' It's one of the most important phrases in Monster-ese because gratitude is very special to us."

Roman and Jude repeated it several times, stumbling over the syllables. "Trumble-grom," Roman finally said, grinning proudly.

"Trumble-grom!" Jude echoed.

They practiced all the phrases, giggling each time they made a mistake, but Mumbles only encouraged them, his whispery voice filled with warmth.

Soon, the boys felt like they were starting to get the hang of it—or so they thought. They decided to test their skills with a conversation. Roman took a deep breath, trying to remember the phrase for "let's have fun."

"Um... Shimmer-wibble-tum?" he said, and immediately burst out laughing.

Jude tried to join in, thinking he remembered the phrase, too. "Sniffle-wizzle-wozz!"

Mumbles chuckled as the boys dissolved into laughter. "Well, that was very close to saying 'Let's have fun and be confused,'" he teased gently.

They tried again, and after a few more failed attempts, they managed to get it mostly right.

"Shimmer-tiddly-tum!" they both shouted, proud of their accomplishment.

"Excellent!" Mumbles said, his soft voice filled with pride. "You're learning faster than I expected."

Encouraged, the boys continued practicing their phrases with Mumbles, each attempt leading to another round of laughter. By the end of their lesson, they had created some unique "monster-ese" phrases of their own, ones that didn't make much sense but filled the room with joy.

When their dad walked in later and heard them saying things like "Snibble-wizzle-frangle!" and "Tum-frangle-tiddly!" he just shook his head, smiling. He didn't understand a word of it, but he could tell his boys were having the time of their lives.

Before Mumbles floated away, he whispered, "Remember, boys, monster-ese is about the feeling as much as the words. So as long as you say it with joy, you're speaking our language just right."

Roman and Jude grinned, feeling like they'd just learned a magical secret. They knew they hadn't mastered monster-ese quite yet, but they'd gotten a lot closer to understanding Mumbles and the wonderful world of monsters.

And they were certain of one thing: Shimmer-tiddly-tum was a phrase they'd be using for a long, long time.

Chapter 8: Backyard Treasure Hunt

It was a sunny Saturday morning, and Roman and Jude were playing outside when they noticed something sparkly near the garden bench. They ran over to investigate and found a small, glittery note pinned to the grass. Jude picked it up carefully, his eyes widening with excitement.

The note sparkled in the sunlight, and written in colorful, swirling letters were the words:

"Shimmer-tiddly-tum! Today's the day for some fun! Follow the clues and hunt with glee; a special prize awaits, you'll see!"

Roman grinned. "It's a treasure hunt!"

Just then, Whiffle appeared in a burst of glitter, giggling with excitement. "Surprise, boys! Today, you're in for an adventure—monster style! We've hidden magical clues all over the backyard. If you can find them all, there's a special prize waiting for you at the end."

Jude's eyes sparkled with excitement. "We're ready! What do we do first?"

Whiffle twirled around, sprinkling glitter in the air. "Just follow the clues, and remember—look carefully! Sometimes the smallest sparkles hide the biggest hints."

Roman and Jude glanced at each other, their faces filled with excitement. They were more than ready to take on a magical scavenger hunt organized by Whiffle and his friends.

"Here's your first clue!" Whiffle said, handing them a small, glittery card. The card read:

"Find the place where veggies grow, where Blinky's glow might start to show."

Roman thought for a moment, then gasped. "The garden! Blinky always liked being around the plants!"

The boys dashed over to the vegetable garden, scanning the area for anything unusual. Near a patch of tomatoes, they saw a faint glow under one of the leaves. They carefully lifted it to find a small, glowing stone, along with another note.

Jude picked up the note, his heart racing. He read aloud:

"Great job! You're on the right track. Next, look where you love to snack!"

Roman and Jude knew exactly where to go next—their favorite spot for snack breaks under the big oak tree. They raced over, and as they approached, they noticed something shiny on the ground. Among the tree roots was a small bag of rainbow-colored popcorn with a tag that read, "Munch's Magical Snack Mix—good for fuelling treasure hunts!"

Roman grabbed the bag and took a bite. "Mmm! This is amazing!"

Jude laughed, grabbing a handful of popcorn. "Best treasure hunt snack ever!"

Blinky floated over, his gentle glow brightening as he watched the boys. "Keep going, boys! You're getting closer."

With renewed energy, the boys read the next clue attached to the popcorn bag:

"Find the place where shadows play, where Mumbles likes to drift all day."

Roman scratched his head, thinking. "Where do shadows play...?"

Jude's face lit up. "The old tire swing! The shadows always fall on it in the afternoon!"

They ran over to the swing and, sure enough, a soft mist seemed to be lingering around it. Mumbles' quiet presence filled the air, and there, tied to the swing, was another glittery note.

Jude read it aloud, smiling.

"Almost there, you're doing great! Now find the place with a hidden gate."

The boys looked around, puzzled. Hidden gate? Roman thought for a moment, then remembered the small wooden gate at the back of the garden that was often hidden behind vines and flowers.

"Come on!" he said, grabbing Jude's arm. "I know where it is!"

They ran to the back of the garden, pushing aside the ivy that hung over the gate. Tied to the gate handle was a sparkling ribbon with a final note.

The note read:

"You've made it, hooray! Now look under the rock for a surprise today!"

Roman and Jude glanced around and saw a large, flat stone right near the gate. With eager hands, they lifted it up—and underneath was a small treasure chest, covered in glitter and sealed with a glowing lock.

"Wow!" Jude whispered, wide-eyed. "This must be the prize!"

Whiffle appeared beside them, clapping his hands with excitement. "You did it! Go ahead—open it!"

Roman lifted the lid, and inside, they found an assortment of magical treasures: a vial of Whiffle's glitter dust, a glow stone from Blinky, a miniature "snack charm" from Munch that was said to make any snack taste better, and a small misty pendant from Mumbles that, according to the tag, would "keep the wearer calm and steady, even in the trickiest of times."

There was also a final note, written in fancy letters:

"Congratulations, Roman and Jude! You've officially completed your first monster-approved treasure hunt. May these magical treasures remind you of the fun we shared today, and of all the adventures yet to come. With love, your monster friends."

The boys beamed, holding up each treasure, admiring the unique qualities of each one. The glow stone pulsed softly in Roman's hand, while Jude shook the vial of glitter dust, watching it sparkle.

"Thank you, Whiffle, Blinky, Munch, and Mumbles!" Roman said, his face full of gratitude. "This was the best treasure hunt ever."

Whiffle grinned, his eyes twinkling with joy. "Anytime, boys! There's always room for more adventures."

As the boys placed their treasures carefully in their pockets, they realized something special—they were no longer just hearing stories about their dad's magical friends. Now, they were making their own.

And with their monster friends by their side, they knew the backyard—and maybe even the whole world—was full of hidden magic, just waiting to be found.

Chapter 9: The Midnight Glow Show

It was nearly midnight, and Roman and Jude lay in their beds, wide awake. They were far too excited to sleep after the thrilling treasure hunt that afternoon. With their new monster treasures tucked safely under their pillows, their minds buzzed with thoughts of more magical adventures. Just as they were about to drift off, a faint glow appeared outside their window.

Roman sat up, squinting into the darkness. "Jude, look! There's a light in the backyard."

Jude rubbed his eyes, peering outside. "Do you think it's…?"

Before he could finish, they heard a soft, familiar voice. "Roman… Jude… come outside!" The whispering tone carried a sense of mystery and excitement.

The boys didn't need another invitation. They threw on their slippers, tiptoed downstairs, and slipped out the back door into the cool night air. The backyard was quiet and still, bathed in soft moonlight. But near the center of the yard, a gentle glow pulsed, lighting up the grass in waves.

As they approached, they saw Blinky hovering in the air, his glow steady and warm. When he noticed them, he brightened, filling the yard with a golden light that felt like a warm hug.

"Hello, boys," Blinky said, his voice soft and welcoming. "I thought you might be up for a little midnight magic. Would you like to see something special?"

Roman and Jude exchanged excited glances, their faces lighting up. "Yes, please!"

Blinky floated higher, his glow growing brighter, and said, "Alright, find a spot to sit, and let's get started!"

The boys quickly settled on a blanket in the middle of the yard, their eyes glued to Blinky. As he floated above them, his glow started to change, shifting from a warm golden hue to a soft blue, then to a shimmering green. The colors blended and swirled together, casting beautiful patterns across the grass and trees.

"Wow..." Jude whispered, his eyes wide with wonder.

Blinky's glow grew brighter, and suddenly, tiny sparks of light began to float around him, like little stars dancing in the air. They drifted toward the boys, swirling around them in a magical embrace, making it feel like they were sitting in the middle of a galaxy.

"This is amazing, Blinky!" Roman said, reaching out to touch one of the glowing orbs. It felt warm and soft, like a gentle breeze that somehow carried light.

Blinky's eyes crinkled with joy as he made the lights dance and pulse, creating waves of color that rolled over the yard like an ocean of stars. He moved gracefully through the air, trailing lights behind him, and soon, the whole backyard looked like it had been transformed into a shimmering, magical world.

"Your dad and I used to do this sometimes," Blinky said, his voice full of fond memories. "When he was feeling down or just needed to relax, I'd put on a little light show. We called it the 'Midnight Glow Show,' and it always cheered him up."

Roman and Jude felt a warm sense of connection to their dad as they imagined him watching a light show just like this one. It was incredible to think that the same magical friend who had brought so much light to their dad was now here, creating memories with them.

"Watch this," Blinky whispered, his glow intensifying as he focused. He began to form the lights into different shapes, creating outlines of stars, hearts, and even a few playful creatures that floated around, winking and waving at the boys before dissolving back into light.

Jude laughed as a glowing bunny hopped toward him before disappearing in a burst of sparkles. "Blinky, this is amazing! How do you make all these shapes?"

Blinky chuckled. "It's all about focus and a little bit of monster magic. Each light is like a tiny friend, willing to play along with whatever I imagine."

As Blinky spoke, he formed the lights into a glittering rainbow arch that spanned the length of the yard. Roman and Jude stared in awe, unable to believe that this magical display was happening right in front of them.

Then Blinky's glow dimmed a little as he floated close to the boys. "Now, would you like to try?"

Roman and Jude's faces lit up. "You mean… we can make the lights move, too?"

Blinky nodded. "I'll help you. Just close your eyes for a moment, and think of a shape you'd like to see. Imagine it clearly, and let yourself feel how excited you are to see it appear."

The boys closed their eyes, concentrating hard. Roman pictured a shining, glowing sun, and Jude imagined a big, fluffy cloud.

"Alright, open your eyes!" Blinky said with a gentle laugh.

When they opened their eyes, there in front of them was a glowing sun and a soft, shimmering cloud, each one floating gently in the air. Roman and Jude gasped, watching their shapes pulse and flicker with life.

"It worked!" Roman exclaimed, his face glowing as brightly as the lights around him.

Blinky chuckled. "That's the magic of believing. You can do anything if you let your imagination lead the way."

The boys continued experimenting, creating shapes and patterns with Blinky's guidance. They made glowing stars, a glittering heart, and even a tiny dragon that soared through the air before bursting into a thousand sparkles.

The Midnight Glow Show went on for what felt like hours, with Blinky creating increasingly intricate patterns, each one more magical than the last. The boys felt like they were in a dream, surrounded by soft lights that danced, floated, and filled the night with warmth.

Finally, as the first hint of dawn began to color the sky, Blinky's glow softened. "It's almost morning," he said, his voice filled with a gentle warmth. "I think it's time to wrap up our show."

Roman and Jude nodded, feeling sleepy but happier than ever. "Thank you, Blinky," Jude said, his eyes heavy with sleep. "This was the best night ever."

Blinky smiled, dimming his glow until it was just a faint flicker. "It was my pleasure, boys. Any time you need a little light, just look for me, and I'll be here."

The boys yawned, their eyes growing heavy as they watched Blinky fade into the early morning mist, his last glow a soft farewell.

As they made their way back inside and snuggled into their beds, they felt a deep sense of peace, as if the magic of Blinky's lights had stayed with them. Just before drifting off to sleep, Roman whispered to Jude, "I feel like we're glowing on the inside, too."

Jude smiled, already half asleep. "Me too, Roman. Me too."

And with that, they slipped into a peaceful sleep, knowing that with friends like Blinky, their world would always be filled with light.

Chapter 10: Monster Hide-and-Seek

It was a lazy Sunday afternoon, and Roman and Jude were sitting in the backyard, still buzzing from their midnight glow show with Blinky. They were hoping for another adventure with their magical friends, and it didn't take long for Whiffle to appear in a burst of glitter.

"Hello, boys!" he said, twirling through the air in a flurry of sparkles. "How about a game?"

The boys' faces lit up. "What kind of game?" Roman asked, sitting up excitedly.

Just then, Blinky, Munch, and Mumbles drifted into view, each one smiling in their own way. Blinky's soft glow pulsed with excitement, Munch was munching on a cracker, and Mumbles gave a soft, whispery chuckle.

"Today, we're playing monster hide-and-seek," Whiffle announced proudly, his voice full of mischief. "It's a favorite among us monsters, and we're quite good at it. But I'll warn you—it won't be easy."

Roman and Jude exchanged excited glances. Hide-and-seek with magical monsters? This was going to be a whole new level of fun!

"Are there special rules?" Jude asked, eager to learn how monster hide-and-seek was played.

Whiffle nodded, his eyes twinkling. "Well, we monsters have a few... tricks up our sleeves. Some of us can turn invisible, and others leave hints, but only if you're paying close attention. Your job is to find each of us!"

Blinky floated closer, his glow dimming until it was barely visible. "Think of it like following little clues. I might leave a faint glow where I've been, but you'll have to look closely."

Munch grinned, crumbs scattering from his mouth. "And I'll probably leave a snack trail. But good luck catching me—I'm fast!"

Mumbles floated softly, his misty form blending into the background. "I'll leave whispers," he said in his gentle, barely-there voice. "If you listen closely, you'll hear me."

The boys were already bursting with excitement. "We're ready!" Roman declared.

Whiffle nodded, grinning. "Alright, boys. Close your eyes and count to ten. Then, come find us!"

Roman and Jude squeezed their eyes shut and started counting loudly, their hearts racing with excitement. They could hear soft giggles, a gentle glow fading, and the faint sound of crunching as the monsters scattered to find their hiding spots.

"Ten!" the boys shouted, opening their eyes. They looked around the yard, scanning for any sign of their magical friends.

The first clue they spotted was a faint shimmer near the garden bushes, sparkling in the sunlight. Roman grinned, recognizing Whiffle's signature trail of glitter.

"Let's start over here," he whispered to Jude, and they tiptoed toward the glittery path.

The trail led them around the side of the house, where a pile of leaves seemed to be moving ever so slightly. Roman and Jude exchanged a knowing smile, and Roman whispered, "Gotcha, Whiffle!"

With a burst of glitter, Whiffle popped up from behind the leaves, laughing. "You're good, boys! But let's see if you can find the others."

Whiffle watched as they moved on, trailing a faint sparkle behind them as they searched.

The boys looked around, trying to spot any other clues. That's when Jude noticed a tiny trail of crumbs leading toward the tree near the swing set. He nudged Roman, pointing at the snack trail.

"Munch has to be close," Jude whispered, and they followed the trail quietly.

As they reached the base of the tree, they heard a faint crunching sound from above. They glanced up and spotted Munch perched on a branch, munching on a cookie, completely unaware he'd been found.

"Found you, Munch!" Roman called up, grinning.

Munch looked down in surprise, quickly shoving the last bite of cookie into his mouth. "Aw, you got me! Guess I left too many crumbs," he chuckled, hopping down from the branch. "But there are still two more to find. Good luck!"

Roman and Jude moved on, scanning the yard for more clues. That's when Roman noticed a faint glow coming from behind a row of flowerpots near the fence. He remembered what Blinky had said about leaving a faint glow as a hint.

"Let's check near the flowerpots," he whispered to Jude.

They crept closer, and sure enough, there was a soft, barely-visible light coming from behind one of the pots. Roman slowly peeked around the edge, and there was Blinky, trying his best to dim his glow.

"Found you, Blinky!" Roman said with a laugh.

Blinky smiled, his glow brightening. "Good job, boys. You're getting the hang of this."

Now, there was only one monster left to find: Mumbles. They knew this would be the trickiest one, as Mumbles had a way of blending into the shadows and drifting through the air without a sound.

"Remember, he said he'd leave whispers," Jude whispered. "Let's listen really carefully."

The boys stood still, closing their eyes for a moment to concentrate. They listened carefully, and then... there it was—a faint, barely-there whisper that sounded like a soft breeze, coming from near the tool shed.

They tiptoed toward the shed, following the whispers that grew ever so slightly louder as they approached. When they reached the side of the shed, they could see a faint, misty shape blending into the shadows.

Roman squinted, focusing hard. "Mumbles... is that you?"

The mist shifted, and a soft chuckle filled the air. Mumbles floated into view, his face a faint smile. "You found me. Well done, boys."

Roman and Jude grinned proudly. They had found every single one of their dad's monster friends, even with their tricky invisibility powers.

"Great job, boys!" Whiffle said, appearing in a burst of glitter. "You've got sharp eyes and good instincts—just like your dad did."

Munch joined in, offering a congratulatory cracker to each of them. "We'll have to make it harder next time," he said with a wink.

Blinky floated over, his glow warm and steady. "I think you've earned the title of honorary monster hide-and-seek champions."

Mumbles drifted close, his whispery voice carrying a note of pride. "And now, you know one of our favorite games. Anytime you're ready for a challenge, we'll be here."

Roman and Jude felt a surge of excitement. This wasn't just any game of hide-and-seek—it was a magical version, filled with clues, glitter, glows, and whispers. It was a game they knew they'd remember forever.

As they headed back to the house, hand-in-hand with their monster friends, they couldn't help but wonder what other magical games and adventures awaited them in the days to come.

Chapter 11: The Case of the Glittery Shoe

It was a perfectly normal morning—or so Roman thought—as he got dressed and headed downstairs for breakfast. But when he looked down to put on his shoes, he noticed something odd. One of his shoes was missing.

"Jude, have you seen my other sneaker?" Roman called out, peeking under the table and behind the chairs.

Jude shook his head, looking equally puzzled. "Maybe you left it outside?"

Roman thought about it, but he was certain he'd brought both shoes in after yesterday's game of monster hide-and-seek. Just then, a soft giggle floated through the air, followed by a faint glimmer of glitter appearing near the kitchen doorway.

Roman and Jude exchanged glances. They knew that giggle well—it was Whiffle.

"Whiffle, is that you?" Roman asked, looking around.

In a burst of sparkles, Whiffle appeared, grinning mischievously. "Good morning, boys! I heard you're missing something?"

Roman sighed, though he couldn't help but smile. "Yes, my shoe! I can't find it anywhere."

Whiffle's eyes sparkled with excitement. "A mystery! Well, lucky for you, I'm an expert in mysteries involving glittery trails and hidden objects."

Jude grinned. "You mean you'll help us find it?"

Whiffle twirled in the air, leaving a swirl of glitter behind him. "Of course! I love a good mystery. Let's get started."

The boys quickly agreed to team up with Whiffle to solve The Case of the Glittery Shoe. Whiffle took on the role of lead detective, with

Roman and Jude as his "junior investigators." They started their search right where the shoe was last seen, near the doorway.

"Now, as any good detective knows," Whiffle began, pacing dramatically, "you have to look for clues. And in our case, clues are usually sparkly!"

Roman and Jude nodded, keeping their eyes peeled for anything unusual. It didn't take long for them to notice a faint glitter trail leading out of the kitchen and into the living room.

"There!" Jude whispered, pointing to the trail. They followed the faint shimmer, crouching low to the ground to keep the trail in sight.

The glitter led them around the couch, across the living room floor, and finally stopped at a small, open closet door. Roman peered inside, half-expecting to see his shoe waiting there, but the closet was empty—except for a few more glittery specks on the floor.

Whiffle examined the area closely, tapping his chin. "Hmm... very curious. It seems someone or something took the shoe from here. Let's keep following the trail!"

The boys followed Whiffle down the hallway, where the glitter trail continued in small patches, almost as if someone had tried to cover it up. They reached the stairs and noticed that the trail went up the steps, glinting faintly as it led them toward the attic.

Roman raised his eyebrows. "The attic? Why would my shoe be up there?"

Whiffle's face was serious, but his eyes twinkled with excitement. "A good mystery always has unexpected twists, my dear Roman. Let's go see what we can find!"

The three of them climbed the stairs to the attic, where they found another clue—a small, sparkly feather stuck to the doorframe. Whiffle examined it carefully, nodding in approval.

"Ah, a feather," he said. "I think I know who might be behind this..."

He led the way into the attic, and there, in the corner, they spotted something surprising: Roman's missing shoe, sitting among a little pile of glitter and feathers.

Roman rushed over and picked up his sneaker. "My shoe! But... why would it be here, with all these feathers?"

Just then, a soft whooo echoed from the rafters, and a small, feathered figure emerged from the shadows. It was Pip, a tiny, mischievous owl monster with big, round eyes and a love for sparkly things.

"Pip!" Whiffle said, grinning. "Caught you red-handed—or should I say, feather-handed?"

Pip blinked innocently, holding up a little glitter-covered feather as if to say, Who, me?

Roman laughed, realizing that Pip must have snuck into the house and been enchanted by the sparkle on his shoe. "Did you borrow my shoe, Pip?"

Pip gave a little nod, his wide eyes filled with mischief, and let out a soft, apologetic hoot. Whiffle chuckled, floating over to Pip and ruffling his feathers.

"Pip has a bit of a weakness for shiny things," Whiffle explained. "And your shoe must have looked too sparkly for him to resist."

Jude laughed, looking at the tiny owl monster. "Well, at least we solved the mystery!"

Pip gave a happy little trill and held out his feather, as if offering it to Roman as an apology. Roman took it with a grin. "Thanks, Pip. I'll keep this feather as a clue from the case of my missing shoe."

Whiffle nodded approvingly. "Well done, junior investigators! We cracked the case and recovered the missing item."

The boys felt a surge of pride, thrilled to have solved their very first monster mystery. As they headed back downstairs, Roman slipped his shoe back on, feeling whole once again. They couldn't help but feel that they'd just experienced one of the silliest—and sparkiest—adventures yet.

Back in the kitchen, Whiffle handed each of them a cookie from Munch's stash, a treat for a job well done. "Here's to more mysteries and plenty of glittery adventures," he said with a wink.

Roman and Jude raised their cookies in a toast, their faces glowing with excitement for whatever sparkly mysteries lay ahead.

Chapter 12: The Monster Snack Recipe Book

It was a rainy afternoon, and Roman and Jude were stuck inside, looking for something fun to do. Just as they were about to start a game, a familiar munching sound echoed from the kitchen. They exchanged a grin—only one monster could make that kind of crunching noise.

"Munch?" Jude called, peeking into the kitchen.

Sure enough, Munch was sitting at the kitchen table with a stack of crackers and a twinkle in his eye. When he spotted the boys, he broke into a big, crumb-covered grin. "Hey there, boys! I was just about to come find you. I've got something special for you today!"

Roman and Jude's faces lit up. "What is it?"

Munch reached into his snack pouch and pulled out a small, colorful book. The cover was decorated with doodles of cookies, crackers, popcorn, and sparkles, and across the top, in big, bubbly letters, it read: "The Monster Snack Recipe Book."

"This," Munch announced proudly, "is the ultimate guide to monster-approved snacks. It has all the recipes for my favorite treats, including a few secret ones your dad and I made up together."

Roman and Jude looked at each other, their excitement building. They'd already enjoyed some of Munch's magical snacks, and now they had the chance to make their own!

"Would you like to try making a recipe?" Munch asked, his eyes twinkling.

"Yes, please!" Roman and Jude said in unison.

Munch flipped through the pages, humming as he scanned the different recipes. "Let's see... Ah, here's a fun one! How about Glow-in-the-Dark Cookies?"

Jude's eyes widened. "Glow-in-the-Dark Cookies? That sounds amazing!"

"Exactly," Munch said, nodding enthusiastically. "These cookies are extra special. Not only are they delicious, but they also glow in the dark thanks to a secret ingredient."

Roman leaned in, curious. "What's the secret ingredient?"

Munch tapped the page in the book. "Glittery glow dust! Don't worry, I've got plenty with me. Now, let's get started!"

The boys gathered the ingredients from around the kitchen, following Munch's directions as he read from the recipe book.

"Alright," Munch said, reading from the page, "Step one: Mix the flour, sugar, and a pinch of magic."

Roman grinned as he added the flour and sugar to a big mixing bowl. "Munch, how much is 'a pinch of magic'?"

Munch chuckled. "Ah, a pinch of magic is different for everyone. But since you're both learning, let's just say it's a big pinch of fun and imagination."

Jude reached into the jar of "glittery glow dust" that Munch had provided, carefully measuring out a small sprinkle. He added it to the bowl, watching as the dough started to sparkle faintly.

"Now, mix it all up!" Munch instructed.

The boys took turns stirring, laughing as tiny sparkles popped up from the dough. The kitchen was soon filled with the warm, sweet scent of cookie dough mixed with a hint of something magical.

"Next, shape the dough into little balls and place them on the tray," Munch continued. "And don't forget to press them down a little with your hands—gives them that special monster-approved shape."

Roman and Jude followed his instructions, pressing each cookie with their palms, creating unique shapes and patterns. Some looked like little suns, while others had swirly designs from their fingertips. As they worked, they noticed that the cookies were starting to glow faintly, as if they were absorbing the light in the room.

"Perfect!" Munch said with a proud smile. "Now, into the oven they go."

They carefully placed the tray in the oven and set the timer. While they waited, Munch told them stories about how he and their dad had experimented with different snacks, from "Rainbow Popcorn" to "Mystery Marshmallow Mountains." Each story made the boys laugh, especially when Munch described the time he and their dad accidentally created a snack explosion in the dorm kitchen.

Finally, the timer dinged. Roman and Jude eagerly opened the oven door, and there, sitting on the tray, were a dozen perfectly baked cookies, each one softly glowing in a range of pastel colors—pale greens, soft blues, and gentle purples.

Munch grinned. "The glow will get even brighter once they cool down a little. Let's take them somewhere dark and see them shine."

They carefully carried the tray to the pantry, turning off the lights and closing the door. In the darkness, the cookies began to glow with a gentle, magical light, each one sparkling with the glittery glow dust they had mixed in.

"Whoa…" Jude whispered, his eyes wide with wonder. "They're glowing!"

Roman picked up a cookie, watching the light dance across its surface. "This is the coolest thing I've ever seen."

Munch chuckled. "And they taste even better than they look! Go ahead, try one."

The boys each took a bite, and their faces lit up with delight. The cookies were soft and sweet, with a hint of magic that made each bite feel like a little burst of joy.

"These are amazing, Munch!" Roman said, licking a few glittery crumbs from his fingers.

Jude nodded, holding up his glowing cookie to get a better look. "Can we try more recipes from the book?"

Munch grinned. "Of course! There are plenty of recipes to keep us busy—like Fizzy Fruit Punch and Popcorn Puffs of Power. Just say the word, and we'll cook up a monster snack storm!"

Roman and Jude couldn't wait to dive into more recipes, but for now, they were content to sit in the cozy pantry, munching on their magical glow-in-the-dark cookies. Each bite was a reminder of the unique friendship they shared with Munch and his world of monster snacks.

As they savoured the last bites, Munch placed the recipe book on the counter with a wink. "Keep this book safe, boys. And remember, the best snacks are made with a little bit of magic and a whole lot of fun."

With their bellies full of glowing cookies and their hearts full of excitement, Roman and Jude knew this was only the beginning of their adventures in the world of monster snacks. They couldn't wait to open the book again and try their hands at more magical treats, with Munch by their side, guiding them every delicious step of the way.

Chapter 13: Mumbles' Invisible Ink

One rainy afternoon, Roman and Jude were playing a quiet game in their room when they heard a soft, familiar whisper drift through the air. They looked around, listening closely.

"Mumbles?" Jude whispered, his face lighting up.

A gentle mist appeared near the window, and Mumbles materialized from the shadows, his translucent form blending into the soft light of the room. "Hello, boys," he whispered with a smile. "I thought you might enjoy learning a little monster trick today. How would you like to learn about... invisible ink?"

Roman and Jude exchanged excited glances. "Invisible ink? That sounds amazing!" Roman said eagerly.

Mumbles nodded, his eyes twinkling with mystery. "Invisible ink is very special to monsters. It allows us to leave secret messages that only certain friends can see. It's great for keeping secrets and forming clubs." He leaned in closer, lowering his voice. "Would you like to make a 'Secret Club of Invisible Messages'?"

The boys nodded enthusiastically. "Yes, please!"

Mumbles smiled, and with a quiet wave of his misty hand, he produced a small vial filled with a shimmery, transparent liquid. "This," he said, "is monster-made invisible ink. Once you write with it, it disappears until you reveal it with a special potion. And the best part? You can make your own!"

He guided the boys to the kitchen, where they gathered simple ingredients to create their own invisible ink. They mixed lemon juice, a pinch of sugar, and a few drops of water in a bowl. Mumbles added a tiny bit of his own misty magic, swirling it in with a gentle breeze, which made the mixture glow faintly for just a moment before becoming clear.

"Now, to write with invisible ink," Mumbles explained, "you just need a cotton swab or a small paintbrush. Dip it in the ink, and carefully write your message on a piece of paper."

Roman dipped the swab in the mixture and carefully wrote a simple message: Hello, Jude!

Jude took his own swab and wrote back: Monster Club Rules!

They both watched as the ink dried, leaving the paper completely blank, with no trace of their messages.

"Now for the best part," Mumbles whispered with a knowing smile. "To read the messages, you need to reveal them with a little heat. Try holding the paper close to a lightbulb, but be careful not to touch it directly."

Roman held his paper up near the desk lamp, his heart racing with excitement. Slowly, as the paper warmed up, faint brown letters began to appear, forming the words Hello, Jude! Roman's face lit up with delight.

Jude tried it with his message, watching as Monster Club Rules! revealed itself, crisp and clear.

"Whoa!" Jude exclaimed. "It really works!"

Mumbles chuckled softly. "Invisible ink is a great way to keep secrets and share messages. You can even hide clues for treasure hunts or write notes that only club members know how to reveal."

The boys loved the idea and immediately set to work making their own "secret club" rules. They grabbed some paper, invisible ink, and a small notebook where they could keep track of their hidden messages.

"Rule number one of the Secret Club of Invisible Messages," Roman announced as he wrote the words carefully in invisible ink, "only club members can read the messages."

Jude nodded, adding his own rule: "Rule number two: Messages can be revealed only when it's very important or very silly."

They continued to make up rules, each one sillier than the last, with Mumbles chuckling along as he watched them get creative. They made up passwords, created secret monster code words like Fogglum Frissle for "hello," and drew little doodles that only the club members would recognize.

"Now, let's test it out," Jude said, dipping his swab in the ink and writing a message for Roman. He handed the paper to his brother with a grin.

Roman held it up to the lamp, eagerly waiting as the hidden message revealed itself. It read: The password to our next meeting is Glitter Cookie.

Roman laughed, loving the silly code word, and quickly wrote a reply: Meet in the backyard fort after dinner for a surprise!

They spent the rest of the afternoon writing invisible notes back and forth, passing messages about future club meetings, secret plans, and silly jokes. Each time they revealed a message, it felt like uncovering a treasure, a hidden connection between them and their new monster friend.

As the sun set and the room filled with shadows, Mumbles gave them each a small vial of his own monster-made invisible ink to keep. "Remember, boys," he said softly, "invisible ink isn't just about hiding words—it's about sharing secrets and trust with those who matter most."

Roman and Jude looked at each other, feeling the weight of his words. This "secret club" wasn't just about invisible ink or hidden messages; it was about building friendships, creating memories, and learning a little more about the magic in their world.

Before Mumbles drifted away, he left them with a final, whispered reminder: "Write your messages with joy, and let your hearts guide your words. The magic will follow."

As the boys lay in bed that night, they each clutched their tiny vials of invisible ink, already thinking of the hidden messages and secret adventures they'd share in the days to come.

And so, the Secret Club of Invisible Messages was officially born, bound by laughter, friendship, and a little bit of monster magic.

Chapter 14: A Monster Campout

Roman and Jude had been begging their parents for a backyard campout, and tonight was the perfect night. The sky was clear, stars were just beginning to twinkle, and a cool breeze rustled the trees. To make it even better, their monster friends had eagerly agreed to join in on the adventure.

The boys helped their dad set up a cozy tent, complete with sleeping bags, flashlights, and plenty of blankets. As soon as the tent was ready, they spotted Whiffle, Blinky, Munch, and Mumbles gathering nearby, each one bringing a bit of monster magic to the evening.

"Are you ready for a night of camping, monster-style?" Whiffle asked with a twinkle in his eye, swirling a bit of glitter in the air.

Roman and Jude grinned. "Definitely!" they said together.

The monsters helped arrange the perfect campfire setting, with Blinky casting a soft glow over the area, Mumbles adding a gentle mist around the tent to make everything feel cozy, and Whiffle sprinkling a light trail of glitter around the firepit. Munch, of course, had brought a large bag filled with snacks, including a special treat he couldn't wait to share: monster s'mores.

Once everyone was gathered around the firepit, Blinky brightened his glow to a warm, flickering light, making it feel like a real campfire.

"Now, what's a campout without s'mores?" Munch announced, pulling out a bag of colorful marshmallows that sparkled with little flecks of glitter.

Roman raised an eyebrow, smiling. "Are those... monster marshmallows?"

Munch nodded proudly. "Indeed! These marshmallows are special—they're enchanted to taste extra delicious, and they glow a little in the dark!"

The boys' eyes widened as Munch handed each of them a stick with one of the magical marshmallows on the end. As they held the marshmallows over Blinky's glow, the marshmallows began to shimmer, casting a soft light across their faces.

Whiffle added graham crackers and pieces of chocolate to the snack spread, explaining, "These aren't just any graham crackers—they're sprinkled with monster glitter for an extra crunch! And this chocolate? Monster-made, rich and gooey."

Roman and Jude assembled their monster s'mores, marveling at how the marshmallows sparkled and glowed between the crackers and chocolate. When they took their first bite, the s'mores were everything Munch had promised—sweet, gooey, crunchy, and a little bit magical.

"These are the best s'mores ever!" Jude said, grinning with chocolate smeared on his face.

"Glad you think so," Munch replied, munching on his own s'more with equal enthusiasm.

Once they'd devoured their monster s'mores, it was time for campfire stories. Whiffle floated closer to the fire, his voice dropping to a playful whisper.

"Alright, who wants to hear the tale of the Glitter Ghost of Galloping Gulch?" Whiffle asked, his eyes wide with excitement.

Roman and Jude leaned forward, eyes wide with curiosity. "We do!" they said, their voices barely above a whisper.

Whiffle launched into a hilarious, slightly spooky tale about a glitter-covered ghost who travelled through monster campsites leaving trails of sparkles wherever he went. The boys were captivated, gasping and laughing as Whiffle described the ghost's antics, including his tendency to cover sleeping monsters with glitter so they'd wake up sparkling.

When Whiffle finished his story, Mumbles drifted forward, his voice a soft murmur in the darkness.

"I have a story, too," Mumbles said. "It's about the Whispering Woods, a place where sounds carry secrets and every breeze holds a message…"

Mumbles' story was mysterious and magical, filled with whispering trees and creatures that communicated through soft sounds and hidden messages. Roman and Jude listened, enraptured, as Mumbles described a night in the Whispering Woods, where he'd heard ancient voices in the trees and learned the secret language of the forest.

When Mumbles finished, the boys looked at each other, feeling as though they'd just been transported to the woods he'd described.

Next, it was Blinky's turn. He shared a story about "The Night of the Floating Lights," describing an adventure where he and their dad had created a light show that filled an entire lake with glowing, floating orbs. The boys could almost see it, picturing their dad and Blinky lighting up the night together, making memories under the stars.

Finally, Munch told a story about a "Monster Feast" that had almost gone wrong when he'd accidentally made too many treats and had to invite every creature in the forest to help him finish them. His story had everyone laughing, especially when he described the tiny forest animals trying to carry huge, glittery marshmallows back to their nests.

As the stories wound down, Roman and Jude leaned back, staring up at the stars, feeling grateful for their magical friends and the unforgettable evening they were sharing. The night was quiet, except for the soft crackling of Blinky's light and the occasional glittery giggle from Whiffle.

Eventually, the boys yawned, feeling the warmth of the blankets and the coziness of the mist that Mumbles had wrapped around the tent.

"Thank you for the best campout ever," Roman said, his voice sleepy but filled with happiness.

Whiffle gave a gentle sprinkle of glitter, his voice soft. "The best campouts are the ones spent with friends."

The monsters each said a quiet goodnight, with Blinky dimming his glow to a soft, nightlight-level warmth that bathed the tent in a comforting glow. Munch handed the boys one last mini s'more each, whispering, "Just a little snack for good dreams."

Mumbles drifted through the air, murmuring a gentle lullaby that felt like a breeze on a warm summer night. The boys closed their eyes, lulled by the sounds of their magical friends and the peace of the night.

As they drifted off to sleep, they knew this campout would be a memory they'd carry with them forever—a night filled with glowing treats, glittery ghost stories, and the warmth of true friendship under the stars.

Chapter 15: Meet Gigglesnort, the Prankster

It was an ordinary Saturday morning in the house—or so Roman and Jude thought. As they made their way down to breakfast, they noticed something unusual. Every few steps, they'd hear a faint snicker, almost like someone was trying to hold back laughter.

"Did you hear that?" Jude asked, glancing around.

Roman nodded, a curious smile spreading across his face. "It sounds like... giggles?"

Just then, a tiny whoopee cushion appeared on the kitchen counter, out of nowhere. Roman poked it, and it gave a loud "pffft!" noise, making both boys burst out laughing.

"Who put that there?" Jude said, looking around.

Before either of them could guess, a small, mischievous-looking creature popped up from behind the fruit bowl. He was round and bouncy, with a big nose, a toothy grin, and eyes that sparkled with pure joy. He wore a small jester hat with bells that jingled every time he moved, and his whole body seemed to wiggle with excitement.

"Allow me to introduce myself!" he announced, his voice full of energy. "I'm Gigglesnort, the master of pranks and tickler of funny bones!"

The boys couldn't stop giggling. Just looking at Gigglesnort made them want to laugh. He had a funny way of moving, bouncing around like he was made of rubber, and every time he did, a small jingle sounded from his hat.

Roman's face lit up. "Did you know our dad?"

Gigglesnort gave a deep, dramatic bow, one hand to his heart. "Oh, indeed! Your dad and I had the best prank battles back in the day. I'd set up silly surprises, and he'd try to guess where the next one would be.

I heard there are new pranksters in the house, so I thought I'd pop in and share a few of my tricks with you two."

Jude's eyes sparkled with excitement. "Are you going to teach us how to prank?"

Gigglesnort wiggled his eyebrows. "Oh, am I ever! But remember, the best pranks are light-hearted and never mean. They're all about spreading laughter, not trouble!"

The boys nodded eagerly, ready to learn the art of pranking.

"Alright," Gigglesnort said with a grin, "let's start with something simple. How about a squeaky sock surprise?"

He pulled out a tiny squeaker from his pouch and slipped it into one of Roman's socks on the floor. "Now, when someone puts that on, they'll hear a little squeak every time they take a step!"

Roman tried it out, slipping his foot into the sock. As soon as he stepped down, a loud squeak filled the room. He took another step, and it squeaked again. Roman and Jude doubled over laughing.

Gigglesnort clapped his hands. "Success! Now let's try a classic: the fake bug trick." He reached into his jester pouch and pulled out a rubber spider, which he handed to Jude.

"Place this somewhere unexpected," Gigglesnort instructed, "like on the bathroom sink or next to the cereal boxes. When someone sees it, they'll get a funny little shock."

Jude ran to place the spider on the bathroom counter, snickering to himself. He could already imagine someone's reaction when they spotted it.

Next, Gigglesnort taught them how to make "prank juice." He showed them how to add a few drops of food colouring to the bottom of a glass and cover it with water, so that when someone poured juice, it would magically change color.

The boys were having the time of their lives, setting up each little prank and laughing along with Gigglesnort's endless supply of tricks.

The house soon became a "giggle zone," as everywhere they looked, there was a new, silly surprise waiting.

In the hallway, Gigglesnort helped them tape a paper cutout of a funny mustache over the family portraits, and they added googly eyes to random objects in the living room. Even Blinky floated by, curious about all the laughter, and ended up with a little sticker on his back that said "I glow in the dark!" Blinky chuckled along, joining in on the fun.

As the final touch, Gigglesnort brought out his "prank masterpiece"—a self-inflating whoopee cushion with glitter. "Now, the trick here," he explained, "is to place it under a pillow or cushion where someone will sit without noticing it. When they do—pffft!—instant giggles!"

The boys carefully placed the whoopee cushion on the couch, barely able to contain their laughter. A moment later, their mom walked by, sat down on the couch, and—PFFFT!—a burst of glitter shot into the air with a loud noise. She looked around in surprise, then burst out laughing as glitter rained down around her.

"Did you two have something to do with this?" she asked, grinning and brushing glitter from her hair.

Roman and Jude pointed at Gigglesnort, who was now bouncing with laughter, rolling around on the floor in delight. "Guilty as charged!" he declared, between fits of giggles.

After a few more rounds of pranks, Gigglesnort gathered the boys and put his hand on his heart. "Now, remember, pranks are for spreading laughter. The best pranksters are the ones who can laugh with everyone, not at anyone."

The boys nodded, understanding the magic behind Gigglesnort's pranks wasn't in tricking people but in bringing joy and laughter to everyone around them.

As the afternoon wound down, Gigglesnort handed each boy a tiny whoopee cushion keychain as a souvenir. "A little reminder that laughter is the best magic of all," he said with a wink.

Before he left, Gigglesnort gave them one last wink. "Anytime you need a good giggle, just call my name, and I'll be there with a new trick up my sleeve!"

With a final, glittery bounce, Gigglesnort disappeared, leaving behind a trail of laughter and memories that the boys would cherish forever. And as they looked around at the googly-eyed decorations, squeaky socks, and surprise bugs scattered throughout the house, they knew they'd turned their home into the ultimate giggle zone—a place where laughter and fun would always be welcome.

Chapter 16: Whiffle's Glitter Dance Party

It was a quiet afternoon when Whiffle appeared in a swirl of sparkles, practically bursting with excitement. Roman and Jude were in the living room, looking for something fun to do, and Whiffle seemed to have read their minds.

"Boys! Are you ready for something spectacular?" Whiffle said, his voice bubbling with energy.

Roman and Jude exchanged curious glances. "What's the plan, Whiffle?"

Whiffle did a little twirl, leaving a trail of glitter in the air. "How about a Glitter Dance Party! A party isn't a party without music, dancing, and a whole lot of glitter!"

The boys' faces lit up. A dance party sounded amazing, especially one with monster-style moves. "We're in!" they shouted, jumping up from the couch.

Whiffle clapped his hands, releasing a small cloud of glitter that shimmered and sparkled as it floated around the room. "Wonderful! Now, the first thing we need is atmosphere. Let's make this place shine!"

With a wave of his hand, Whiffle sent glitter swirling through the air, covering the living room with a soft, shimmering glow. The glitter settled on the furniture, walls, and floor, giving everything a magical sparkle. Even the lamp shades sparkled, creating little rainbows that bounced around the room.

Next, Whiffle held up his hands and summoned a small, floating disco ball that spun slowly, casting spots of light everywhere. "Perfect!" he said with a grin. "Now, for the music!"

With a snap of his fingers, a lively beat filled the room, the kind that made you want to start dancing the second you heard it. Whiffle began to sway to the music, his body moving in fun, wiggly ways that made Roman and Jude laugh.

"Alright, boys," Whiffle called, "it's time to learn some monster moves! First up: The Glitter Shuffle. Watch closely!"

Whiffle demonstrated the Glitter Shuffle, sliding his feet side-to-side with little hops and twists, leaving a trail of glitter with each step. He shimmied his shoulders, wiggled his fingers, and did a little twirl that scattered glitter in a circle around him.

Roman tried the move, laughing as he left his own glitter trail behind. "I think I've got it!"

Jude joined in, adding a little spin to his steps, making his glitter fly in all directions. "This is so much fun!"

Whiffle beamed, delighted to see the boys catching on so quickly. "Now, for the Sparkle Spin! This one's all about twirling and letting the glitter fly. Just hold your arms out, spin as fast as you can, and let the sparkles go wild!"

The boys spread their arms and spun in circles, giggling as the glitter danced around them, creating little sparkly clouds. They felt like they were inside a giant snow globe of glitter.

"Perfect!" Whiffle cheered. "Now, for the final move—the Monster Boogie!" He started bouncing from side to side, moving his arms up and down like he was stirring a giant, invisible pot. "This one's all about letting loose. Go big, go silly, and make as much glitter as you can!"

Roman and Jude copied Whiffle's moves, bouncing and boogieing around the room. The three of them danced together, moving from the Glitter Shuffle to the Sparkle Spin and then to the Monster Boogie, laughing all the way.

The living room soon became a glitter-filled dance floor, with sparkles floating in the air and the music pulsing around them. The boys even added their own moves, like the "Twinkle Twist" (a twisty spin with extra glitter) and the "Shimmer Stomp" (a big stomp that sent glitter flying up in a burst).

Just then, Blinky and Munch appeared, drawn by the music and laughter. "What's going on in here?" Blinky asked, his glow brightening as he took in the sparkly scene.

"It's a dance party!" Jude exclaimed, grabbing Blinky's hand and pulling him onto the "dance floor."

Munch, never one to miss out on fun (or snacks), joined in, wiggling his way over and adding his own "Munch Mambo" to the mix. Each time he moved, a few crumbs flew into the air, which only made everyone laugh harder.

Before long, even Mumbles appeared, drifting quietly into the room. At first, he seemed shy, but with a little encouragement from Whiffle, he started floating in gentle loops, adding a graceful, misty dance to the party. His movements were soft and slow, like a whisper in the wind, and as he floated, tiny, silvery sparkles followed him, creating a magical contrast to the lively glitter.

The monsters and boys danced together, mixing their moves, sharing laughs, and having the time of their lives. The room was filled with sparkle and glow, with each monster's unique magic adding to the dazzling effect.

As the music slowed down, they all collapsed onto the couch, breathless and grinning from ear to ear. Glitter floated gently down around them, settling on their hair, clothes, and the cushions, leaving everyone looking like they'd been dipped in stardust.

"That," Jude panted, "was the best dance party ever."

Whiffle nodded, his own face flushed with joy. "You two are excellent dancers! I think you've mastered the art of monster moves."

Blinky chuckled, his glow still pulsing with excitement. "I've never seen so much glitter in one place!"

Munch grinned, reaching into his snack pouch and pulling out a few crackers. "Dance parties make me hungry! Anyone else need a snack?"

They all laughed, reaching for crackers and resting together in their glittery living room, feeling happy, tired, and completely covered in sparkles.

As the boys snuggled into the couch, they realized this wasn't just any dance party—it was a memory they'd keep forever. Thanks to Whiffle, they'd had a magical, glitter-filled night, and they knew there would be many more monster parties to come.

Before heading off, Whiffle gave them each a small packet of glitter dust. "Keep this handy, boys. Whenever you need a little extra sparkle, just sprinkle some and dance like monsters!"

Roman and Jude clutched their glitter packets, already planning their next glitter dance party. As they watched Whiffle and the others disappear in a swirl of sparkle, they knew their house had officially become a place where magic, laughter, and dance moves would always have a home.

Chapter 17: The Glow-Stone Adventure

It was just after dusk, and the last light of the sun was fading, casting the backyard in soft shadows. Roman and Jude were sitting on the back porch, admiring the first stars appearing in the sky, when they noticed a gentle glow coming from the far end of the yard. They squinted, trying to see what it was, and soon made out Blinky's familiar, comforting light floating toward them.

"Good evening, boys," Blinky said, his glow warming the cool night air. "I thought tonight would be perfect for a little adventure."

Roman and Jude exchanged eager glances. "What kind of adventure?" Roman asked, leaning forward in excitement.

Blinky smiled, his glow flickering like a candle. "We're going on a treasure hunt to find something very special—a glow stone. It's a magical stone that holds a soft light, perfect for guiding you in the dark or giving you a little extra courage when things feel uncertain."

Jude's eyes widened. "A glow stone? That sounds amazing! Did our dad ever have one?"

Blinky nodded, his face filled with fond memories. "Yes. I gave him one back when he was in college. Whenever he needed a bit of light—whether he was studying late or feeling homesick—he could hold his glow stone, and it would bring him peace. I thought it might be time for you two to find one of your own."

Roman and Jude stood up, buzzing with excitement. "We're ready!" they said together, eager to begin the hunt.

"Excellent," Blinky said, floating higher. "Now, the glow stone is hidden somewhere in the backyard. I left a few clues to help you find it, and I'll be right here to guide you. Let's get started!"

The boys nodded, and Blinky led them to the first clue, which he had hidden near a large tree at the edge of the yard. As they approached, they noticed a faint shimmer near the roots—a small note written in glowing ink.

Jude picked up the note and read it aloud:

"Where the flowers bloom by day and rest at night, there lies a path to the glow stone's light."

Roman thought for a moment, then grinned. "The flower garden! It has to be!"

Blinky nodded approvingly. "Very clever, Roman. Let's head to the garden."

They made their way to the flower beds, where the night-blooming flowers were just beginning to open. Soft moonlight lit up the petals, making them look almost enchanted. As they searched among the flowers, they spotted another shimmering clue tucked under a daisy.

Jude picked it up, holding it close to Blinky's light so they could read it.

"Next, look for a place where shadows fall, a hiding spot for one so small."

Roman and Jude glanced around, considering all the spots where shadows might be. Then Jude snapped his fingers. "The garden gnome! It's always hiding in the shadows under the bushes!"

They ran to the small garden gnome statue nestled between two bushes. When they got there, Blinky's glow revealed a faint shimmer on the gnome's hat, where another clue was waiting.

Roman unfolded the tiny note, reading:

"Find the spot where water flows, where secrets rest and magic grows."

Jude's face lit up. "The birdbath! That's where the water flows!"

The boys dashed over to the birdbath, scanning it carefully. As they peered inside, Blinky's glow reflected off a small object at the base—a stone unlike any they'd seen before. It was round and smooth, with a faint, soft light shining from within, like a captured star.

Roman picked it up carefully, his eyes wide with awe. "This... is this the glow stone?"

Blinky smiled, his glow warming with pride. "Yes, Roman. That is a glow stone. It will always provide a gentle light when you need it, just like the one I shared with your dad."

Jude held out his hand to touch the stone, feeling its warmth and gentle energy. "It's so beautiful... like it's alive."

Blinky nodded. "In a way, it is. Glow stones carry a bit of my light with them, so that wherever you go, you'll have a piece of magic to guide you. Remember, you don't need to see the whole path—just a little light is enough to show the way."

The boys held the glow stone together, feeling its warmth and the quiet, reassuring light that seemed to fill them with peace. They realized that this stone wasn't just a magical object; it was a reminder of their new friends, of the adventures they'd shared, and of the wonderful surprises waiting in the world around them.

"Thank you, Blinky," Roman said, holding the glow stone close. "We'll keep it safe, and we'll always remember this night."

Jude nodded in agreement, his face filled with gratitude. "Yeah, and we'll use it whenever we need a bit of light."

Blinky's glow softened, as if he were smiling. "That's exactly what it's for, boys. And any time you need more than a glow stone, remember I'll be here."

As the night grew darker, the boys and Blinky headed back toward the house. Roman kept the glow stone in his pocket, feeling its gentle warmth even through the fabric. It was comforting, like having a small piece of Blinky with them wherever they went.

When they reached the back porch, Blinky gave them each a small hug, his glow brightening one last time before dimming gently.

"Goodnight, boys. May your paths always be bright," he whispered, drifting away into the shadows with a final, soft glow.

Roman and Jude watched him disappear, holding their glow stone as they headed back inside. They knew they'd always have Blinky's light with them now, not just in the stone but in their hearts, guiding them through any darkness they might face.

As they drifted off to sleep that night, the glow stone rested beside their bed, casting a soft light over the room. And just as Blinky had promised, it filled their dreams with warmth, courage, and the gentle magic of friendship.

Chapter 18: Monster Snow Day

Roman and Jude woke up to a magical sight—the entire backyard was covered in a thick blanket of snow, sparkling under the winter morning sun. The trees were dusted with white, and everything looked like it had been touched by a winter fairy.

"Snow day!" Roman shouted, jumping out of bed.

Jude was already grabbing his coat and mittens, his face glowing with excitement. "Come on! Let's go make a snowman!"

As the boys bundled up and ran outside, they heard soft, familiar giggles and saw tiny puffs of glitter floating in the cold air. Whiffle appeared in a swirl of sparkles, his face bright with excitement.

"Good morning, boys! It looks like today is a Monster Snow Day!" Whiffle announced, twirling around and leaving a trail of glitter in the snow.

Just then, Munch, Blinky, and Mumbles joined them, each one marveling at the snowy wonderland. Munch pulled out a thermos of hot cocoa, Blinky glowed softly, casting a warm light on the white landscape, and Mumbles floated quietly, admiring the beauty of the snow.

Roman's face lit up. "Are you guys here to play in the snow with us?"

Whiffle nodded enthusiastically. "Oh, yes! We monsters love a good snow day. In fact, I think it's time for a little monster-style snow fun!"

The boys cheered, ready for whatever snowy adventure their monster friends had planned.

First Stop: Sledding

Whiffle led the way to a hill at the back of the yard. Munch had brought a few colorful sleds that sparkled in the sun, each one dusted with a bit of monster magic. Roman and Jude hopped on the sleds, holding tight as Whiffle gave them a little push.

"Ready... set... go!" Whiffle shouted, sending them zooming down the hill, with glitter flying off the sleds like a trail of stardust.

The boys laughed as they raced each other, the sleds gliding smoothly over the snow. Blinky floated alongside them, his glow casting a magical light on the path, making the snow glitter even more brightly.

Munch, of course, had packed snacks for the ride down the hill. Every time they reached the bottom, he handed out a small cookie or a bite of warm cinnamon bread, fuelling them up for the next slide down.

"Best sledding ever!" Jude exclaimed as he zoomed down again, leaving a trail of glitter behind him.

Next Up: Snow Forts

After sledding, Whiffle suggested they build a snow fort. The boys and monsters worked together, rolling large snowballs and stacking them to form walls. Munch was surprisingly good at shaping the snow, and with his help, they soon had a sturdy fort complete with snow towers and tiny snow windows.

Blinky added a magical touch by placing small glow stones on top of the walls, casting a soft light that made the fort look like a magical castle.

"This is the coolest snow fort ever!" Roman said, grinning as he admired their creation.

Whiffle giggled. "Just wait—there's one more thing we need." He sprinkled a handful of glitter over the fort, making it sparkle as if it were enchanted. The whole structure gleamed in the sunlight, like something out of a winter fairy tale.

The Glittery Snowball Fight

Just as they were admiring their fort, Whiffle's eyes sparkled mischievously. "Now, what's a snow day without a snowball fight?"

Roman and Jude laughed, immediately scooping up snowballs. Whiffle was already forming a stash of glittery snowballs, and he winked before throwing the first one, which exploded in a burst of sparkles on Roman's jacket.

"Oh, it's on!" Roman laughed, tossing a snowball back at Whiffle, who dodged it with a giggle.

The boys and monsters launched into a full-scale snowball battle, with glitter flying everywhere. Blinky and Mumbles teamed up, Blinky creating glowing snowballs that left soft, shimmering trails and Mumbles crafting misty snowballs that seemed to disappear and reappear in the air.

Munch, true to his nature, paused now and then to snack on the snow, adding his own trail of cookie crumbs to the glitter and snow around him.

Roman and Jude couldn't stop laughing as they dodged glittery snowballs and tossed their own, covering each monster in snow and sparkles. Whiffle was an expert at dodging, but every now and then, the boys managed to catch him with a snowball, which only made him giggle harder.

In the middle of the battle, Jude suddenly shouted, "Snow monster alert!" and formed a giant snowball, rolling it toward the fort. Roman quickly helped, adding even more snow until they had created a massive snow creature right in front of their fort.

Whiffle clapped his hands in delight, adding a sprinkle of glitter to the snow monster's head. "There! A perfect guardian for our fort!"

Warming Up with Monster Hot Chocolate

As the snowball fight wound down, Munch called everyone over for a special treat. He had brought a big thermos of monster hot chocolate, which he poured into small cups. The hot chocolate was extra thick and topped with marshmallows that shimmered in different colors.

"Here you go!" Munch said, handing each of them a cup. "This is my special Glittery Hot Chocolate, perfect for warming up after a snowball fight."

Roman and Jude took a sip, and their faces lit up with delight. The hot chocolate was rich, creamy, and had a hint of cinnamon and vanilla, with marshmallows that seemed to melt in their mouths in a burst of flavour.

"This is amazing, Munch!" Roman said, taking another sip.

Munch beamed, clearly pleased. "It's a monster favorite. And it makes for the perfect ending to a snowy adventure!"

As they sat together, sipping hot chocolate and admiring the snow-covered backyard, Roman and Jude felt a deep warmth, both inside and out. They'd had the best Monster Snow Day ever, complete with sledding, snow forts, glittery snowballs, and magical hot chocolate.

Whiffle smiled at them, his face glowing with happiness. "Remember, boys, even the coldest days can be filled with warmth and laughter when you have friends by your side."

The boys nodded, snuggling into their coats, their hearts full of joy and their cheeks flushed from the fun.

As the sun began to set, casting a warm glow over the snowy landscape, the monsters bid the boys goodbye, promising that they'd be back for many more snowy adventures.

And as Roman and Jude headed inside, their hands still warm from their cups of hot chocolate, they knew this Monster Snow Day would be a memory they'd treasure forever.

Chapter 19: The Glitter Bomb Incident

It was a Saturday afternoon, and Roman and Jude were exploring Whiffle's collection of magical trinkets in the living room. Their favorite thing about Whiffle's belongings was that every item seemed to have a special sparkle or shimmer to it. Among the collection, one small, brightly coloured ball caught their attention. It was smooth and round, with flecks of glitter swirling inside like a tiny galaxy.

"What do you think this is?" Jude whispered, carefully picking up the glittery ball.

Roman leaned in, his eyes wide with curiosity. "I'm not sure. Maybe it's just a decoration?"

Just then, Whiffle appeared beside them, his eyes widening as he saw the boys holding the small ball. "Oh, boys, be careful with that!" he said, trying to keep his tone light but clearly concerned. "That's one of my glitter bombs. They're only supposed to be used for special celebrations."

Jude and Roman's faces lit up with excitement. "A glitter bomb? What does it do?"

Whiffle grinned sheepishly, as though caught with a secret. "It's a little… well, it's like a big burst of glittery fun. When you set it off, it creates an explosion of sparkles that covers everything around it. But it can get quite messy, so I only use them on special occasions!"

Jude's eyes sparkled with mischief as he glanced at Roman. "Just imagine… a whole room covered in glitter!"

Roman giggled, already imagining the sparkly mess. But before they could ask Whiffle for a demonstration, Jude accidentally pressed a small button on the glitter bomb, and a faint click sounded from within the ball.

Whiffle's eyes went wide. "Oh no! Boys, get ready—it's about to go off!"

Before they could react, the glitter bomb exploded in a brilliant, swirling cloud of sparkles, filling the entire kitchen with an explosion of glitter. The air was thick with shimmering flecks of every color, and it looked like a glittery snowstorm had hit.

For a moment, the boys stood frozen in surprise, watching as the glitter rained down, covering the countertops, cabinets, and floor in a thick layer of sparkles. The sunlight streaming through the window made the room glisten like a rainbow.

Jude burst into laughter, holding out his hands and watching as the glitter covered his arms and clothes. "We're covered! Everything's covered!"

Roman looked around, equally amazed. "Whiffle, this is incredible! It's like we're inside a giant snow globe!"

Whiffle couldn't help but laugh, though he looked a bit sheepish. "Well, that's the power of a glitter bomb! It's fun, but it's definitely a mess." He twirled around, leaving a small trail of glitter in the air. "This kitchen won't forget this day anytime soon!"

The boys began dancing around the kitchen, tossing handfuls of glitter into the air and leaving trails of sparkles everywhere they stepped. It wasn't long before they started a mini glitter fight, flinging handfuls of it at each other, turning the kitchen into a full-on glitter explosion.

"Okay, maybe this wasn't supposed to happen... but it's the best mess ever!" Jude declared, his face beaming.

Just then, their mom walked into the kitchen and stopped in her tracks, her eyes widening as she took in the glitter-covered scene. "What... happened in here?"

Roman and Jude paused, looking sheepishly at each other, then back at their mom.

"It was a glitter bomb," Roman explained, trying not to laugh. "We accidentally set it off."

SAMMY'S MONSTERS AND THE MAGIC OF ROMAN & JUDE

Their mom's initial shock melted into a grin as she took in the sight of her sons, completely covered in glitter, and Whiffle, who was equally sparkly and floating nearby with a guilty smile.

"Well," she said with a sigh, "I suppose every kitchen could use a little extra sparkle once in a while."

The boys cheered, grateful for her good-natured response. Whiffle floated closer, looking around at the glitter-covered kitchen. "I promise I'll help clean up," he said with a wink. "But let's have a little more fun first!"

With that, Whiffle spun around, creating a small glittery whirlwind, and the boys joined him, dancing and laughing as they played in the glitter-filled room.

Eventually, they began cleaning up, with Whiffle showing them a bit of monster magic to make the glitter "disappear" more quickly. He used a small enchanted feather duster, which whisked the glitter into little piles that floated up and vanished with a soft pop. Even cleaning was fun when Whiffle was around.

By the time they finished, there was still a hint of glitter left behind—a sparkle here, a shimmer there. The kitchen had a faint, magical glow, a reminder of the unexpected glitter explosion.

As they stepped back to admire their work, Jude grinned. "The kitchen will never look the same again, but I think it's better this way."

Roman nodded, brushing the last bit of glitter from his hair. "Totally worth it."

Whiffle smiled proudly. "That's the spirit, boys. A little bit of glitter can turn any day into something special."

The boys hugged Whiffle, thanking him for the sparkiest adventure yet, and with a final, mischievous sprinkle of glitter, Whiffle disappeared, leaving them with memories of a glittery mess, plenty of laughs, and a kitchen that would shimmer with magic for days to come.

Chapter 20: The Invisible Chalk Drawings

One quiet afternoon, Roman and Jude were playing in the backyard when they noticed a faint mist drifting toward them from the far side of the garden. As it came closer, they recognized the soft, whispery form of Mumbles.

"Hello, boys," Mumbles greeted them in his gentle, airy voice. "I thought today might be perfect for a bit of invisible art. Would you like to learn how to create drawings that only we monsters can see?"

Roman and Jude's faces lit up with excitement. "Invisible art? That sounds amazing!" Roman said eagerly.

Mumbles floated closer, pulling out a small, misty pouch. From it, he took out two pieces of chalk that looked ordinary but shimmered faintly in the sunlight, as if made from fog and light. "This is invisible chalk," he explained, his voice soft but filled with excitement. "To humans, it looks like nothing at all, but to monsters, it's like the brightest colors of the rainbow. We'll be able to see every detail of your artwork."

The boys took the chalk, examining it closely. It felt soft and cool in their hands, almost like holding a tiny cloud. They could hardly wait to get started.

"Let's create something together," Jude suggested, his eyes wide with inspiration.

Mumbles nodded approvingly. "How about a mural on the fence? It can be our secret masterpiece—only visible to us and your monster friends."

Roman and Jude grinned, feeling like they were about to embark on a magical mission. They chose a spot along the wooden fence, where they had plenty of space to create their hidden artwork.

"Remember," Mumbles said as he handed them each a piece of chalk, "the invisible chalk responds to your imagination. Think about what you want to draw, and let the chalk bring it to life."

The boys nodded, letting their imaginations run wild. Roman started by drawing a big sun with swirling rays, imagining it glowing brightly, while Jude added a few fluffy clouds and a rainbow that stretched across the sky. Although the drawings looked completely invisible to them, they trusted that Mumbles could see everything.

"This is so cool," Jude said, adding stars to the sky, imagining them twinkling with hidden magic.

Mumbles floated beside them, watching their creations come to life. "Wonderful! I can see every detail—the sun, the clouds, the stars. It's like a hidden world you're creating."

Encouraged by Mumbles' words, the boys continued adding to the mural. Roman drew a magical forest with trees that seemed to reach up to the stars, their branches filled with invisible creatures that he imagined were tiny, friendly monsters. Jude added a winding river that sparkled as it flowed, imagining it filled with glowing fish and enchanted plants.

Before long, they had filled the fence with a secret world of hidden magic. There were glittery flowers, mysterious mountains, and even a small castle perched on a hill, with little invisible flags waving in the imaginary breeze.

"What else can we add?" Roman asked, standing back to admire their work, even though they couldn't see it.

Mumbles floated closer, his face filled with admiration. "How about we add something to welcome your monster friends?"

The boys thought about it, then together, they wrote a message at the top of the mural: "Welcome, Monsters! Enjoy our secret masterpiece."

When they were finished, Mumbles gave a soft, joyful laugh. "It's incredible! You boys have created a magical place, full of color and life.

It's a secret mural only we can see, but it's filled with all the wonders you imagined."

Roman and Jude stepped back, feeling a sense of pride in their invisible creation. Even though they couldn't see it, they knew their mural would be there, waiting to be discovered by their monster friends.

"Thank you for showing us this, Mumbles," Jude said, grinning. "I think this might be our best art project ever."

Mumbles nodded, his whispery form shimmering with pride. "It's my pleasure, boys. Invisible art is a special gift—only those with imagination and a bit of magic can truly appreciate it."

As the sun began to set, Blinky, Whiffle, and Munch wandered over, curious about the boys' mysterious project. Blinky's glow brightened as he gazed at the mural, his eyes widening with delight.

"Whoa, this is amazing!" Blinky said, his light pulsing with excitement. "I can see the rainbow, the castle, and even the little creatures in the trees! You two have real talent."

Whiffle floated closer, his face lighting up with joy. "Look at this forest! I've never seen such an imaginative place. It's like a hidden world come to life."

Munch grinned, admiring the magical river Jude had drawn. "And the welcome sign! Now every monster knows they're invited to enjoy this masterpiece."

The boys beamed, thrilled that their monster friends loved the mural as much as they'd hoped. They spent the rest of the evening showing their friends around their invisible artwork, describing the parts they couldn't see and sharing the stories behind each detail.

As the stars began to twinkle overhead, Mumbles gave each boy a tiny piece of invisible chalk to keep. "This is for whenever you want to add to your masterpiece, or start a new one," he said softly. "Art like this never fades, because it lives in the imagination."

Roman and Jude took their chalk with grateful smiles, feeling like they had been entrusted with a magical tool. They promised to add more to the mural, to let it grow and change, creating a hidden world that only the monsters and those with a touch of magic could see.

Before they left, the boys and their monster friends gathered one last time by the mural, taking in the beauty of their shared secret.

"Every time we pass by this fence, we'll know there's something magical here," Roman said, feeling a special warmth in his heart.

"And maybe someday, we'll add even more to it," Jude added, imagining a mural that stretched across the whole yard.

As they said goodbye to Mumbles and their friends, Roman and Jude knew they had created something truly unique—a secret masterpiece that would live on in their memories and in the hidden corners of their backyard.

And as they drifted off to sleep that night, they dreamed of their magical mural, knowing that it was out there, glowing brightly under the stars, waiting for the next touch of invisible chalk and the next spark of imagination.

Chapter 21: Munch's Marshmallow Mountain

It was a chilly evening, and Roman and Jude were reading on the couch when they heard a familiar rustling sound coming from the kitchen. They exchanged a grin—there was only one monster who could make that much noise with snacks.

Sure enough, Munch waddled in, carrying an enormous bag filled with marshmallows of every size, shape, and color. His eyes sparkled with excitement, and his cheeks were already dusted with a bit of powdered sugar.

"Boys!" Munch exclaimed, his voice filled with enthusiasm. "I've got a plan, and it's going to be the tastiest adventure you've ever been on."

Roman's and Jude's faces lit up. "What's the plan, Munch?" Jude asked, bouncing on the couch.

Munch gave them a dramatic pause, then held up a giant marshmallow in each hand. "We're going to build a Marshmallow Mountain! A tower of marshmallows, right here in the living room!"

The boys cheered, already envisioning the mountain of fluff. Roman immediately got down on the floor, ready to help with whatever marshmallow magic Munch had in mind.

"Let's make it huge!" Jude said, already pulling the smaller marshmallows out of the bag.

Munch grinned. "That's the spirit! We'll start with the jumbo marshmallows as the base, and then we can add layers and layers of smaller ones. Oh, and don't worry—I've got plenty of marshmallows."

With that, they got to work. They began by laying out the largest marshmallows in a big circle on the floor to form the base. As they stacked more and more marshmallows, the mountain began to take shape. It was a glorious tower of fluff, with marshmallows of all colors and sizes piled high in wobbly layers.

Munch took a break to munch on a few marshmallows as he worked, tossing a handful to each of the boys. "Building takes a lot of energy," he explained, popping another marshmallow in his mouth.

After a while, Whiffle floated in, drawn by the laughter and the sweet smell of marshmallows. "What's all this?" he asked, his eyes twinkling as he took in the scene.

"It's Marshmallow Mountain!" Jude explained, tossing a marshmallow up to Whiffle, who caught it with a giggle. "Want to help us?"

Whiffle nodded eagerly, sprinkling a bit of glitter over the marshmallows as he worked. "A little sparkle will make it even more magical!"

With Whiffle's glitter and Munch's endless supply of marshmallows, the mountain grew taller and wider, until it looked like a sugary, fluffy volcano about to erupt. Each marshmallow seemed to glow under the sparkle, creating a sweet, glittery wonderland.

Just then, Blinky floated in, his glow brightening as he saw the towering mountain. "Whoa, that's incredible! But don't you think it needs a final touch?"

He reached into his glow pouch and pulled out tiny, colorful glow stones, placing them carefully around the mountain so it sparkled and shimmered in a rainbow of colors.

Roman's eyes widened. "It's like a real mountain, only better! It even has little 'gems' in it!"

Munch stepped back, admiring their work, his face beaming with pride. "It's perfect. And now, we climb!"

The boys and monsters took turns "climbing" the mountain, carefully placing their hands and feet on the marshmallows to reach the top. With each step, they squished into the soft marshmallows, laughing as they nearly lost their balance on the fluffy peaks.

Finally, Munch reached the top, striking a triumphant pose. "I hereby declare this Munch's Marshmallow Mountain!" he announced, his voice echoing with pride.

Roman and Jude joined him at the top, sitting among the marshmallows as if they were on a mountaintop, looking out over their living room kingdom. The mountain wobbled slightly under them, but that only made it more fun.

Then, Munch pulled out his last surprise—a bottle of chocolate sauce. "And now, for the tastiest part of the adventure!"

He drizzled chocolate sauce down the sides of Marshmallow Mountain, making it look like lava flowing down from the peak. The boys cheered as the chocolate sauce ran over the marshmallows, coating everything in delicious gooeyness.

"Best. Mountain. Ever!" Jude declared, grabbing a marshmallow coated in chocolate.

They all began to dig in, each one finding marshmallows dipped in chocolate or covered in glitter. Whiffle giggled as he tasted one of the sparkly marshmallows, and Blinky's glow pulsed with joy as he munched on a marshmallow near one of his glow stones.

"This is the tastiest adventure we've ever had," Roman said, savouring a gooey marshmallow.

Munch nodded, his cheeks stuffed with marshmallow. "A marshmallow mountain is the best kind of mountain. Tasty and fun!"

They continued to snack on the marshmallows, each bite filled with laughter and a bit of sticky chocolate. By the time they were done, Marshmallow Mountain had dwindled to a small, sparkly hill, with everyone covered in marshmallow fluff and chocolate smudges.

As they sat back, full and happy, Whiffle sprinkled a bit more glitter over them all. "A mountain of memories made in one sweet day," he said with a twinkle in his eye.

The boys and monsters laughed, knowing they'd just shared one of the most magical (and delicious) days they'd ever had.

And as they cleaned up the remains of Marshmallow Mountain, they promised that the next adventure would be just as sweet, with friends who made every mountain feel like the top of the world.

Chapter 22: Meet Nibbles, the Tiny Snack Monster

It was a sunny afternoon, and Roman and Jude were playing in the backyard when they spotted Munch walking toward them, carrying a small pouch of snacks as usual. But this time, he wasn't alone. Bouncing along beside him was a tiny creature with big, bright eyes, a round belly, and a smile that seemed way too big for his little face.

"Boys, I'd like you to meet my cousin, Nibbles," Munch said proudly, giving the tiny monster an affectionate pat on the head. "He's got a big appetite and an even bigger knack for finding snacks."

Nibbles grinned up at Roman and Jude, his little fangs gleaming. He was only about a foot tall, but he had an energy that seemed to make him twice his size. His body was covered in soft fur, and he wore a little red scarf that made him look extra friendly.

"Hi, Nibbles!" Roman said, bending down to shake his tiny paw. "Nice to meet you!"

Nibbles gave a little squeak of excitement and quickly sniffed Roman's hand, his nose twitching as if he were searching for a hidden snack.

Jude giggled. "Does he smell snacks on everything?"

Munch chuckled. "Oh, you'd be surprised! Nibbles can sniff out a snack from a mile away. He once found an entire jar of peanut butter hidden under a bed in just a few minutes."

Nibbles puffed up with pride at the compliment, his big eyes sparkling with enthusiasm. Without waiting another second, he began darting around the yard, his nose leading him as he searched for any snack remnants or hidden treats.

The boys watched in amusement as Nibbles explored every nook and cranny, poking his head under bushes, behind rocks, and even inside an old flowerpot.

"What's he looking for?" Roman asked, laughing as Nibbles pulled his head out of a flowerpot with a satisfied grin.

"Anything edible," Munch explained with a smile. "Nibbles has a gift for finding the tastiest surprises in the most unexpected places. And he loves sharing his discoveries."

Sure enough, Nibbles soon returned with a small packet of crackers he'd found at the bottom of the flowerpot, holding it up triumphantly for the boys to see.

"Where did that even come from?" Jude asked, amazed.

Munch shrugged, clearly impressed with his little cousin's skills. "Nibbles has a way of finding things that even I don't notice."

Nibbles eagerly tore open the cracker packet and offered one to each of them, clearly pleased to share his find. The boys each took a cracker, touched by the tiny monster's generous spirit.

After a few minutes of munching, Nibbles' ears perked up, and he darted toward the back porch, sniffing as he went. He scrambled under the porch steps, disappearing for a few seconds, then popped out with a small chocolate bar, which had apparently been lost there ages ago.

"Wow! He's like a treasure hunter for snacks!" Roman exclaimed.

Nibbles bounced with excitement, clearly enjoying his role as "Snack Finder Extraordinaire." He placed the chocolate bar in front of the boys like a prized trophy, watching eagerly as they unwrapped it.

As they enjoyed Nibbles' latest find, Munch looked on proudly. "Nibbles has been training to be a snack hunter since he was little. He's got a special gift for sniffing out even the tiniest treat. We used to call him 'The Snack Seeker' back home."

Nibbles squeaked happily, clearly proud of his title. Then, as if to prove himself further, he darted over to a nearby bush and returned holding a small bag of chips, which he laid at their feet like another treasure.

Jude clapped, laughing. "Nibbles, you're amazing! Do you want to help us hide some snacks so we can do a treasure hunt with you?"

Nibbles' eyes grew wide with excitement, and he bounced in place, nodding eagerly.

The boys quickly gathered a few small snacks from the kitchen and carefully hid them around the backyard, tucking them behind trees, under rocks, and even in the branches of bushes. Nibbles watched them hide each snack, his tiny nose twitching with excitement.

When they finished, Munch gave Nibbles a gentle nudge. "Alright, cousin, time to show them what you've got!"

With a happy squeak, Nibbles began his hunt, moving quickly from one hiding spot to the next, his nose leading him to each snack as if by magic. He found the treats hidden in the bushes, the ones behind the rocks, and even the cracker they'd hidden high in the branches.

"He's unstoppable!" Roman said, cheering as Nibbles uncovered the last hidden snack, a small bag of gummies tucked inside a hollow tree stump.

Nibbles squeaked in triumph, holding up the bag of gummies with a proud grin. He passed it to Roman and Jude, clearly pleased to share his spoils.

As they sat down to enjoy the final treat, Nibbles climbed into Jude's lap, curling up happily with a marshmallow Munch had handed him as a reward. Jude patted Nibbles' soft fur, feeling grateful for his new friend's incredible snack-finding skills.

"You're the best snack hunter ever, Nibbles," Jude said, scratching behind his tiny ears.

Nibbles squeaked in response, closing his eyes with a satisfied smile. Munch sat down beside them, watching his little cousin with pride. "Nibbles has a big heart to match his big appetite. I knew you'd love him."

Roman and Jude shared a smile, realizing that Nibbles was a perfect addition to their monster family. With a knack for finding hidden treats and a generous spirit that made every snack taste a little sweeter, Nibbles had made their afternoon one they'd never forget.

As the sun set, casting a warm glow over the backyard, the boys, Munch, and Nibbles sat together, surrounded by wrappers and crumbs—a sure sign of a "tastiest adventure" well-spent. And as they shared one last round of snacks, they knew that, with Nibbles around, every snack hunt would be an unforgettable treasure hunt.

Chapter 23: A Glittery Art Show

It was a rainy afternoon, and Roman and Jude were stuck indoors, feeling a little bored. Just as they were deciding what to do, Whiffle popped into the room, leaving a trail of sparkles in his wake.

"Boys, what do you say to a bit of glittery art magic today?" Whiffle asked with a mischievous twinkle in his eye.

Roman and Jude perked up immediately. "What do you mean, Whiffle?" Jude asked, curious.

Whiffle pulled out a handful of glitter in every color imaginable, letting it rain down like confetti. "I'm talking about an art show! You two can make your very own masterpieces, and I'll bring a bit of monster magic to each one. When we're done, we'll have a glittery family art show right here in the living room!"

The boys beamed with excitement, already imagining their artwork sparkling with Whiffle's magical touch.

Soon, Mumbles, Blinky, and Munch arrived, each one bringing a bit of their own magic to the project. Blinky had glowing paints, Mumbles brought misty stencils, and Munch carried glittery, snack-shaped stamps. They were ready to turn the living room into an art studio!

Step One: The Backgrounds

They started by laying out large sheets of paper on the floor. Whiffle handed Roman and Jude brushes, encouraging them to get creative with the backgrounds.

Roman decided to paint a sky scene, mixing blue and white to create fluffy clouds. With Blinky's glowing paint, he added touches of orange and pink to look like a sunrise, making the sky come alive with color.

Jude went for an enchanted forest, painting tall, dark trees with faintly shimmering leaves. Mumbles floated over, placing misty stencils on the paper to create ghostly, soft shapes between the trees, adding a mysterious vibe.

"Looking good, boys!" Whiffle said, nodding in approval. "Now for some glitter."

He handed each boy a small, enchanted brush that sprinkled glitter wherever they painted. Roman added silver glitter to his clouds, while Jude made the leaves of his trees sparkle with emerald green. The backgrounds sparkled beautifully, each one now shining with its own unique magic.

Step Two: Magical Details

With the backgrounds complete, it was time for the details. Blinky hovered nearby, adding tiny glow stones to Roman's sunrise, which made the painting shimmer as if the sun were truly rising on the page.

"Whoa, it's like it's alive!" Roman whispered, watching the tiny stones pulse with soft light.

Jude decided to add a river winding through his enchanted forest. Munch handed him a special stamp that left glittery, wave-like impressions, making the water sparkle as it "flowed" through the trees.

Mumbles floated over and added a misty effect to the trees, creating a gentle fog that gave Jude's forest a mystical, otherworldly look. "It's like a secret forest," Jude said, grinning. "I love it!"

Step Three: Finishing Touches

With the main parts of their artwork complete, Whiffle suggested they add personal touches to each painting. He encouraged them to think of something that would make their art truly unique.

Roman decided to add little birds in the sky, using a tiny glitter brush to paint them in delicate strokes. Blinky added a few glow spots around the birds, making them look like they were flying through beams of morning light.

Jude chose to add enchanted creatures hidden among the trees. He used Mumbles' stencils to paint faintly glowing foxes and rabbits peeking out from behind the trees, giving his forest a magical, lively feel.

Munch, meanwhile, added one last special touch to each piece: tiny snack shapes—cookies, marshmallows, and tiny candy stars—tucked subtly into the background. Roman and Jude laughed as they spotted the little snacks hidden in their own artwork.

The Art Show Begins

Once they finished, Whiffle, Blinky, Mumbles, and Munch helped set up their art show in the living room. They hung the glittery paintings on the walls and arranged soft lights around each piece to make them sparkle even more.

When their mom walked in and saw the glitter-filled art show, her eyes widened with delight. "Wow! This is incredible! Did you boys make all of these?"

Roman and Jude nodded proudly, their faces glowing with excitement.

"It's our Glittery Art Show," Jude explained. "And our monster friends helped us add some magical touches!"

Their mom walked slowly around the room, admiring each piece. She pointed to Roman's sunrise and smiled. "It looks like it's actually glowing!"

"That's thanks to Blinky!" Roman said, grinning as Blinky gave a proud glow beside him.

When she reached Jude's enchanted forest, she gasped, noticing the mist and the glowing creatures peeking out from behind the trees. "Jude, this forest looks like a fairy tale! It's beautiful."

Jude beamed. "Mumbles helped with the mist, and Munch added a few hidden snacks!"

Their dad joined in, looking equally amazed. "This is a magical art show," he said, inspecting each detail. "You've created something truly special."

As a final touch, Whiffle gave each piece a light dusting of sparkle, making the entire room feel like it was filled with stardust. The paintings shimmered and glowed, casting rainbows around the room.

A Magical Keepsake

Before they wrapped up the art show, Whiffle presented Roman and Jude with a small, glittery keepsake. It was a tiny book filled with invisible chalk and enchanted paper, allowing them to draw new magical art whenever they liked.

"This is so you can always make more art," Whiffle explained. "Even when we're not here, you'll have a little bit of our magic to add to each piece."

The boys hugged Whiffle and their other monster friends, feeling grateful for the amazing day of art and magic.

That evening, as they sat around admiring their glittery art show with their parents, they knew they had created something more than just artwork—they'd made a memory they would cherish forever, filled with the colors, sparkles, and laughter of their magical friends.

And even after the art show came down, they kept their tiny magical book, knowing it held the power to bring a touch of monster magic to their everyday world.

Chapter 24: Glow-in-the-Dark Hideout

One chilly evening, Roman and Jude were in their room, trying to think of a new adventure. As they looked around for inspiration, they heard a soft, familiar glow and felt a gentle warmth behind them.

Blinky was floating nearby, his light casting a soft glow over the room. "Hey, boys," he said with a friendly smile. "How would you like a secret hideout—one that glows in the dark?"

Roman's and Jude's eyes lit up. "A glow-in-the-dark hideout? That sounds amazing!" Roman exclaimed.

Blinky chuckled, clearly pleased by their excitement. "I thought so! And the best part is, we can make it right here in your closet. It'll be a cozy, magical space just for you two."

The boys quickly cleared out a corner of their closet, moving aside a few clothes and shoes to make room. Blinky floated in, inspecting the space and nodding approvingly.

"First things first, let's get some magical lighting in here," Blinky said, his glow pulsing slightly as he concentrated. He reached into his glow pouch and pulled out a handful of tiny, glowing stones, each one softly pulsing with a different color.

"These are glow stones," Blinky explained, handing them to the boys. "They'll light up your hideout with a gentle, cozy glow."

Roman and Jude helped Blinky arrange the glow stones around the closet, sticking them to the walls and the ceiling. The stones emitted a soft, colorful light that bathed the closet in shades of blue, green, and purple, making the small space feel like a magical cave.

"Wow, it's already starting to look like a secret hideout!" Jude whispered, his face glowing with excitement.

Making It Cozy

Next, Blinky suggested they add some comfy pillows and blankets to make the hideout cozy. The boys grabbed a few of their softest pillows and a fluffy blanket, arranging them to create a little nest in the corner. Blinky added his own special touch by draping a small, glowing shawl over the top of the closet, making it feel like a canopy of stars above their heads.

"Every hideout needs a comfy spot to sit," Blinky said, settling onto a pillow. "And the more pillows, the better!"

Roman and Jude climbed into the nest of blankets and pillows, testing out their new hideout. It felt warm and cozy, like a little cocoon of light and comfort.

Adding the Glow Effects

Blinky then reached into his glow pouch again, pulling out a jar of special "glow dust." He opened it carefully, showing them the sparkly, luminescent powder inside. "This is glow dust. Just a pinch will make anything glow, like a gentle, soft starlight."

Blinky sprinkled a bit of glow dust on the ceiling of the closet, creating tiny specks that looked like stars. As he blew gently on the dust, it spread out in a swirl, creating a galaxy of softly glowing lights above them.

Roman stared up at the glowing "stars," feeling like he was lying under a magical sky. "It's beautiful, Blinky! It feels like we're in outer space."

Jude smiled, reaching up to touch one of the glowing stars. "This is the best hideout ever!"

Blinky chuckled softly. "Every hideout needs a bit of magic. And there's one more thing we can add to make it even better."

A Touch of Monster Magic

With a playful smile, Blinky reached into his pouch one last time, pulling out a small, enchanted crystal that shimmered with a soft, golden light. "This crystal is special. It can create a 'mood glow' that changes colors depending on what you're feeling."

He placed the crystal in the center of the closet, and immediately it started glowing a warm, cheerful yellow. The boys watched in awe as the light shifted to green, then to pink, each color filling the closet with a different feeling of warmth and happiness.

"Wow," Roman whispered, captivated by the changing colors. "It feels like the whole room is alive."

Jude reached out to hold the crystal in his hands, feeling its gentle warmth. "It's like having a little piece of magic with us, no matter what."

Blinky smiled, his own glow softening with pride. "Exactly. This hideout is now your secret, glowing escape—a place where you can read, imagine, or just relax in your own magical world."

The First Adventure in the Hideout

Once the hideout was complete, the boys couldn't wait to spend time in it. They grabbed their favorite books, snuggled into the blankets, and turned on a small, portable speaker to play soft music. Blinky floated nearby, adding a gentle glow that brightened whenever they laughed or gasped at a story twist.

They spent hours in the cozy space, reading and laughing, sometimes just lying back and watching the glow stone "stars" twinkle above them. The magical hideout quickly became their new favorite spot—a place filled with soft light, warmth, and the feeling of safety that only a true secret hideout could provide.

After a while, Mumbles peeked into the closet, drawn by the glow. "What's going on in here?" he whispered, his misty form blending into the soft lights.

"We made a glow-in-the-dark hideout with Blinky!" Roman explained, showing Mumbles around. "It's like our own magical clubhouse."

Mumbles floated in, settling comfortably among the pillows. "It's wonderful. It feels like a dream world in here."

As the evening went on, Whiffle and Munch also joined, turning the hideout into a cozy gathering spot. They shared stories, snacks, and a few rounds of silly jokes, each monster adding their own unique magic to the space.

A Place of Magic and Comfort

By the time their parents called them for dinner, Roman and Jude didn't want to leave their hideout. It had become a special place, filled with memories and magic, thanks to Blinky and their monster friends.

Before they left, Blinky placed a small charm over the hideout—a tiny glowing amulet that would keep the glow stones lit even after he left.

"Now your hideout will always have a little bit of light, even when I'm not here," he said, smiling.

The boys hugged Blinky, thanking him for helping them create the most magical space they could ever imagine.

That night, as they drifted off to sleep, they couldn't stop thinking about their glow-in-the-dark hideout, knowing it would always be there for them—a hidden world of light, comfort, and monster magic, ready to welcome them anytime they needed a little escape.

Chapter 25: The Backyard Obstacle Course

It was a warm, sunny day, and Roman and Jude were in the backyard, looking for something fun to do. Suddenly, they heard a burst of giggles and the unmistakable sound of glitter scattering in the air.

Whiffle appeared, swirling around them in a cloud of sparkles, with Munch, Blinky, and Mumbles close behind, each carrying mysterious items.

"Hello, boys!" Whiffle said with a twinkle in his eye. "How would you like to take on the Monster Backyard Obstacle Course? It'll be full of challenges, surprises, and a few magical twists."

Roman and Jude cheered, jumping up with excitement. "Yes! What kind of obstacles are there?"

Whiffle grinned mischievously. "Only the silliest, glitteriest, and snack-filled obstacles you've ever seen!"

With the monsters' help, they began setting up the course. Each monster contributed their own unique touch, creating a truly magical backyard adventure.

Step 1: The Glitter Tunnel

Whiffle's first obstacle was a long, sparkly tunnel made of tall cardboard tubes lined up end to end, decorated with rainbow glitter inside and out.

"To make it through the glitter tunnel," Whiffle explained, "you have to crawl on your hands and knees—and try not to get too sparkly!" He winked, knowing that was impossible.

The boys took turns crawling through, and by the time they reached the other side, they were covered head to toe in glitter, laughing as they shook off the sparkles.

Step 2: The Glow Stone Hop

Next up was Blinky's obstacle. He had scattered glow stones across the lawn, each one pulsing with soft, colorful light.

"To pass this challenge, you have to hop from stone to stone without touching the ground," Blinky instructed, his glow flickering with excitement. "But be careful—some stones will flash if you stay on them too long!"

Roman and Jude started hopping, trying to step lightly on each glow stone. As they moved, the stones would flash beneath their feet, lighting up like a colorful dance floor. They had to stay on their toes, hopping quickly to avoid the flashing stones. By the time they reached the end, they were laughing and breathless.

Step 3: Munch's Snack Station

Halfway through the course, Munch had set up a "snack station," complete with mini tables filled with treats. There were tiny sandwiches, sparkly marshmallows, and glitter-covered popcorn in small paper cones.

"To continue, you have to snack up for energy!" Munch announced proudly. "But remember, only a few bites—there's more course ahead!"

The boys grabbed a couple of snacks, laughing as they tried the glittery popcorn, which seemed to shimmer with every bite. The marshmallows tasted sweet with a hint of magic, giving them an extra boost of energy.

Step 4: Mumbles' Misty Maze

The next obstacle was created by Mumbles, who had set up a maze of misty barriers in a zigzag pattern across the yard. As he floated around, he left trails of gentle fog that hovered at knee level.

"To pass through my maze," Mumbles explained in his soft, whispery voice, "you'll have to zigzag without stepping out of the mist. If you do, you'll have to start over!"

The boys stepped into the maze, carefully weaving their way around the foggy trails. Mumbles made it tricky by floating just ahead of them, creating new misty barriers as they moved. It was like walking through a dream, and they loved every moment.

Step 5: The Sparkle Slide

Whiffle had saved the silliest obstacle for last. At the far end of the yard, he had set up a small slide covered in glitter that led to a pit of soft, sparkly foam blocks.

"To finish the course, you have to slide down the Sparkle Slide and land in the Glitter Pit," Whiffle said, grinning. "And remember, you can't avoid the glitter this time!"

Roman and Jude climbed to the top of the slide, feeling like they were about to dive into a pool of stardust. They pushed off and whooshed down the slide, landing in the foam pit, which exploded with glitter as they hit the bottom.

They emerged from the pit covered in sparkles, looking like they'd been dipped in pure magic. Munch cheered, and Blinky's glow brightened as they completed the final obstacle.

Victory Celebration: Glitter Medals and Snacks

As Roman and Jude climbed out of the foam pit, Whiffle held up two glittery medals on strings. "Congratulations, boys! You've completed the Monster Backyard Obstacle Course!" he said proudly, placing a medal around each of their necks.

Blinky floated over, adding, "You both did amazing! You're now official members of the Monster Adventure Team!"

Munch handed them each a final snack—marshmallow pops dipped in chocolate and rolled in edible glitter. "A victory snack for the champions!"

The boys bit into their treats, savouring the sweetness, while Mumbles created a soft mist that made the entire yard feel like a magical hideaway.

The Aftermath: A Backyard Full of Magic

After the celebration, the boys and the monsters sat on the grass, taking in the scene. The glow stones, the sparkly tunnel, and the glitter pit transformed the backyard into a magical playground.

Roman smiled, looking at his glitter-covered arms and his glowing medal. "That was the best obstacle course ever!"

Jude nodded, still catching his breath from the maze and the slide. "I didn't think it could be so magical—and silly!"

Whiffle laughed, throwing one last handful of glitter in the air. "That's what we do best, boys! Silly, sparkly, and full of surprises!"

As the sun set, casting a golden glow over the yard, Roman and Jude knew they would remember this day forever. Their backyard had transformed into a world of magic and laughter, a place where anything was possible with a little monster magic and a lot of imagination.

And as they walked inside, still covered in glitter and wearing their victory medals, they were already dreaming of the next adventure.

Chapter 26: Monster Pyjama Party

One evening, as the stars began to twinkle in the sky, Roman and Jude decided to host something they'd always wanted to do—a pyjama party for their monster friends! They rushed to gather blankets, pillows, and snacks, making sure everything was perfect for a night filled with fun and laughter.

Before long, Whiffle, Munch, Blinky, and Mumbles arrived, each one in their own version of "pyjamas." Whiffle had on a sparkling nightcap that seemed to sprinkle glitter wherever he went, Blinky had wrapped himself in a soft, glowing shawl that pulsed with a gentle light, Munch had a snack pouch tied around his waist, and Mumbles wore a misty blanket that floated around him like a soft cloud.

"Welcome to our pyjama party!" Roman said, greeting each monster with a big smile.

"Tonight's going to be amazing!" Jude added, holding up a bowl of popcorn covered in sparkly sugar for a magical twist.

The monsters cheered, and Whiffle clapped his hands, creating a burst of glitter in the air. "Oh, I brought a little something special for tonight—a pile of my famous glittery pillows! They're perfect for pillow forts and comfy enough for the best pyjama parties."

Whiffle reached into his magical bag and pulled out an array of pillows that shimmered with glitter. Each pillow was fluffy and soft, covered in sparkles that changed colors depending on the light. Roman and Jude grabbed a few, testing how bouncy they were and laughing as glitter puffed out with each bounce.

"Alright, let's build the ultimate pillow fort!" Roman declared.

Everyone worked together, stacking the glittery pillows in a circle and draping blankets over the top. They added soft cushions and cozy blankets inside, creating a magical hideaway that glowed with Blinky's light and sparkled with Whiffle's glitter. When they were done, it looked like a mini castle made of fluff and sparkle.

"Best pillow fort ever," Jude said, crawling inside and settling into a comfy spot.

With the fort complete, Munch brought over his snack station, loaded with popcorn, cookies, and hot chocolate with tiny marshmallows. Each drink was topped with a sprinkle of edible glitter, making them look like the most magical hot chocolates ever.

The group snuggled into the fort, munching on popcorn and sipping hot chocolate as they laughed and shared stories. Whiffle led them in a game of "Monster Truth or Dare," with questions like "What's the silliest thing you've ever done?" and dares like "Sing your favorite song while doing the Glitter Shuffle." By the end of the game, everyone was laughing so hard they could barely breathe.

After a few rounds of games, Blinky suggested they tell spooky, silly stories. The glow monster dimmed his light, casting a soft, shadowy glow around the fort. Whiffle began with a tale about a "Glitter Ghost" who went around spooking monsters by sprinkling glitter on their noses. Munch shared a story about the "Hungry Phantom" who visited monster kitchens at night, eating all the best snacks.

As each story was told, Blinky brightened and dimmed his glow, making shadows dance around the fort, which only added to the thrill of each story. Mumbles even added a spooky mist, making it feel like they were in a real ghost story. Each monster and the boys took turns making their best "ooooo" sounds, and every story ended in giggles instead of gasps.

Finally, as the night wore on, Whiffle brought out one last surprise—a pile of glittery pillows that he called "dream pillows." "These pillows are special," he explained, handing one to each friend. "When you sleep on them, they give you the best dreams ever."

Roman and Jude hugged their dream pillows, which sparkled faintly in the dim light of the fort. They settled down, feeling the cozy warmth of the pillows and the happiness of having their monster friends around them. With Blinky casting a gentle, star-like glow, everyone snuggled in and closed their eyes.

As they drifted off to sleep, Roman and Jude felt like they were floating in a sea of glitter and dreams, surrounded by the love and laughter of their friends. It had been the best pyjama party they could have ever imagined—filled with stories, laughter, magic, and the soft sparkle of a night shared with friends.

And as the night turned to morning, the fort stood as a cozy reminder of the night's magic, with a sprinkle of glitter on every pillow and the warmth of friendship filling the air.

Chapter 27: Mumbles and the Ghostly Giggles

It was a quiet, misty evening, and Roman and Jude were sitting on their beds, wondering what kind of adventure they could have indoors. As if on cue, a soft, whispery voice drifted through the room, and Mumbles appeared, floating gently near the window, his misty form blending perfectly with the dim light.

"Hello, boys," he said in his gentle, almost ghostly voice. "How would you like to hear some ghostly giggles and tales of friendly spirits tonight?"

Roman and Jude's faces lit up with excitement. They loved Mumbles' soft, mysterious magic and knew they were in for a special treat.

"Yes, please!" Roman said eagerly.

Jude added, "We'd love to hear your stories, Mumbles. And ghostly giggles sound amazing!"

Mumbles floated over, settling onto a soft pillow on the floor, his misty form creating an eerie, magical glow around him. "I'll tell you a few stories of the Friendly Spirits," he said, his voice soft and soothing. "They're not scary spirits—just gentle, playful ones who like to make others laugh and smile."

He held out his hand, and with a gentle wave, tiny ghostly forms began to appear, floating around the room like soft clouds. They shimmered with a gentle glow, each one carrying a faint giggle that made the boys smile.

"These are ghost giggles," Mumbles explained, chuckling softly. "They're little bits of laughter left behind by happy spirits. When you hear them, they make you feel warm and joyful."

The ghost giggles floated around the boys, filling the room with a sound that was somewhere between a whisper and a laugh. It wasn't loud or spooky—instead, it was soft and soothing, like the gentle rustling of leaves in the wind.

As the giggles floated around them, Mumbles began his first story.

The Story of the Midnight Tickler

"There once was a friendly spirit named Tickle, who visited children only at midnight," Mumbles began. "Tickle was known for her gentle ways, but she had one favorite prank. Just as children were about to drift off to sleep, she'd float by and give their feet the lightest tickle, just enough to make them giggle in their dreams."

Roman and Jude giggled at the thought of a playful spirit tickling sleepy children. They imagined the tiny ghost giggles floating around were little remnants of Tickle's nighttime visits.

"She never wanted to scare anyone," Mumbles continued. "She only wanted to bring a bit of joy and laughter, even in dreams."

Mumbles released a few more ghostly giggles into the air, and they drifted around the room, swirling in gentle loops and making soft, happy sounds. The boys felt a warm comfort settle over them, like they were wrapped in a blanket of laughter.

The Tale of the Whistling Winds

Mumbles began his second story, his voice just above a whisper. "In the forest, there's a place where the wind whistles and sings, even when no one else is around. That's where the Whistling Spirit lives. He loves creating music from the wind, and sometimes, he lets his laugh travel along with the breeze, so that anyone who listens can feel a bit of joy."

Jude leaned forward, enchanted by the idea of a spirit making music in the woods. "What does his laugh sound like?" he asked.

Mumbles created a soft, whistling sound, letting it drift around the room. It was a delicate, lilting sound, like a happy tune carried on the wind. The boys could almost imagine the Whistling Spirit hiding in the trees, playing music just for them.

Mumbles smiled. "Whenever you hear the wind whistle, remember, it may just be the Whistling Spirit saying hello."

The Gentle Glow of Luna, the Light Spirit

Finally, Mumbles told them about Luna, a spirit who brought light to dark places. "Luna would visit places that felt lonely and fill them with a gentle glow. She left behind bits of her own light, so anyone who felt scared or sad could find comfort in her presence."

As he spoke, Mumbles created a soft, glowing mist that filled the room with a warm, cozy light. The boys felt like they were surrounded by a gentle hug.

"Luna's light was so soft that sometimes people would mistake it for a nightlight. But those who really believed in her magic could feel her comfort, even on the darkest nights."

Roman and Jude sighed with contentment, feeling the warmth of Luna's light all around them. The glowing mist made the room feel like a safe, magical place, filled with peace and gentle laughter.

The Magic of Ghostly Giggles

After the stories, Mumbles encouraged the boys to try catching the ghostly giggles. Each time they reached out, the giggles would float just out of reach, making soft, playful sounds. Every giggle they tried to catch left a trace of warmth in the air, like a lingering hug.

"It's amazing how laughter and joy can stay around, even after it's shared," Mumbles said, watching the boys play. "That's what these ghostly giggles are—a reminder of all the happy moments left behind by friendly spirits."

Roman and Jude took turns holding their hands out, watching as the giggles danced around them, creating tiny sparkles as they floated through the air. They realized that the ghost giggles were more than just sounds—they were like tiny treasures, filled with memories of happiness.

When the giggles finally settled down, Mumbles floated close and placed a small, misty charm on each of their nightstands. "These charms will keep a bit of ghostly laughter near you. Whenever you feel lonely or a little scared, just give it a gentle shake, and you'll hear a giggle to make you smile."

Roman and Jude hugged Mumbles, thanking him for the magical evening.

"Tonight was perfect, Mumbles," Roman said, holding his misty charm close.

Jude nodded. "Yeah, I don't think I'll ever be scared of ghost stories again."

Mumbles smiled, his misty form shimmering. "Remember, boys, not all spirits are scary. Some only want to bring comfort, laughter, and a little magic to the world."

As they settled into bed, the boys could still hear the faint sound of the ghostly giggles drifting around the room. With the soft glow of Mumbles' mist and the warmth of his stories, they drifted off to sleep, knowing they were surrounded by the joy and laughter of friendly spirits.

Chapter 28: Blinky's Light Show in the Rain

It was a rainy afternoon, and Roman and Jude were sitting by the window, watching as raindrops pattered against the glass. The grey clouds and steady drizzle had turned the backyard into a misty wonderland, but the boys felt a bit disappointed—outdoor adventures didn't seem possible with all the rain.

Just then, Blinky floated into the room, his glow soft and warm, casting a cheerful light in the otherwise dim space. He noticed the boys' glum faces and smiled knowingly.

"Feeling a bit down because of the rain?" Blinky asked, his glow flickering gently.

Roman sighed. "Yeah, we wanted to play outside, but it's too wet."

Blinky chuckled, a hint of mischief in his voice. "What if I told you that rainy days are perfect for a magical light show?"

Jude perked up. "A light show? In the rain?"

Blinky nodded, his glow brightening. "Yes! The raindrops make perfect lenses for light. With a little monster magic, we can turn this stormy day into something dazzling."

The boys' faces lit up with excitement as they followed Blinky to the back porch, where they could watch the rain from under the shelter. The grey clouds rolled above them, and the rain continued to fall steadily, creating small puddles and ripples across the yard.

"Alright," Blinky said, his glow pulsing with excitement, "watch closely, and keep your eyes on the raindrops."

He floated forward and closed his eyes in concentration. Slowly, his soft yellow glow transformed into a rich, shimmering blue. As his light touched the raindrops, each droplet seemed to capture the color, creating tiny blue glimmers across the yard.

The boys watched in awe as Blinky's blue glow danced in every raindrop, making it look like the entire yard was filled with tiny blue stars.

"Whoa, it's beautiful!" Roman whispered, captivated by the shimmering blue rain.

Blinky then changed his light to a bright, warm green. Instantly, the blue in the raindrops faded, replaced by a soft green glow that sparkled in the puddles and glistened on the leaves. The entire backyard looked like an enchanted forest, with green "fireflies" floating on every surface touched by the rain.

Blinky winked at the boys. "Now, let's add a little more magic."

He began to change colors faster, shifting from blue to green, then to pink, and finally to a warm golden yellow. Each raindrop seemed to change in time with him, turning the backyard into a kaleidoscope of colors, with raindrops glowing like tiny jewels scattered across the grass.

The boys laughed in delight, feeling as if they were in the middle of a magical rainstorm where every drop was alive with color and light.

Jude reached his hand out, letting the raindrops fall onto his palm. "They look like little colorful gems!" he said, grinning as he watched the drops shimmer and glow in his hand.

Blinky smiled, his glow shifting to a soft rainbow, blending all the colors together. "That's the magic of rainy days—they can turn into something amazing when you add a bit of light."

With a twinkle in his eye, Blinky began to float higher, casting his light over the whole yard. The raindrops in the air started to catch his rainbow glow, creating an effect like a thousand tiny prisms floating in the mist. Each droplet refracted the light, scattering rainbows across the yard, the trees, and even the boys' faces.

Roman and Jude looked around in awe, watching as rainbows danced on every surface, filling the entire space with color and magic.

"This is incredible, Blinky!" Roman exclaimed, turning to catch a reflection of the rainbow glow in a puddle.

Blinky beamed, his light growing brighter. "There's one last trick I've been saving," he said, lowering his voice to a conspiratorial whisper.

He floated down closer to the puddles, casting a rich, deep purple light. As his glow touched the puddles, the water's surface seemed to ripple with purple waves, each one glowing like a magical pool. The boys could see their reflections, surrounded by shimmering purple light, as if they were looking into a mystical portal.

Jude leaned over a puddle, enchanted by the swirling purple light. "It's like looking into a magical pond!"

Blinky chuckled softly. "Rainy days hold more magic than you'd think. All it takes is a bit of light to bring it out."

The boys spent the rest of the afternoon watching Blinky's light show, marveling as he changed colors and created different effects with each glow. They laughed as raindrops turned pink, gasped as puddles shimmered gold, and sat in awe as rainbow prisms floated through the air like tiny pieces of magic.

By the time the rain stopped, the sky had begun to clear, and the first rays of the setting sun peeked through the clouds. Blinky's glow softened as he settled back down on the porch with the boys.

"That was the best rainy day ever," Roman said, still in awe of the magical display.

Jude nodded, his eyes wide with excitement. "I'll never think of rainy days as boring again."

Blinky's glow softened to a gentle, contented yellow. "Remember, boys, there's magic in the everyday—sometimes all it takes is a little light to see it."

As they headed inside, Roman and Jude felt like they'd just experienced a new kind of magic, one that made even the greyest day feel bright and special. And from that day on, every time it rained, they'd look out the window and imagine Blinky's colorful glow turning each raindrop into a tiny, sparkling gem.

Chapter 29: Munch's Mystery Snack Mix

It was a cozy afternoon, and Roman and Jude were sitting in the living room, wondering what to do next, when Munch waddled in with a big, covered bowl and a gleam in his eye.

"Hello, boys!" Munch greeted them, his voice filled with excitement. "I've got something special planned for today—a little game I call Munch's Mystery Snack Mix!"

Roman and Jude perked up, their curiosity immediately piqued. "Mystery snack mix?" Jude asked, eyeing the covered bowl eagerly. "What's in it?"

Munch grinned mischievously. "Ah, that's the game! I've put together a mix of different treats and snacks, each with its own unique flavour and texture. The challenge is to guess each ingredient with your eyes closed."

The boys laughed, ready to take on Munch's tasty challenge. "This sounds awesome!" Roman said, already imagining what kinds of treats Munch might have hidden in the bowl.

Munch reached into his pouch and pulled out two colorful blindfolds, handing one to each of them. "You'll need these! Close your eyes and let your taste buds do the guessing."

Roman and Jude put on the blindfolds, settling into their seats and trying not to giggle with excitement. Munch's snack mix games were always delicious, but this one sounded especially fun.

"Alright," Munch said, his voice full of anticipation. "Here comes the first ingredient! Open your mouths, and no peeking!"

The boys opened their mouths, and Munch placed a small piece of something crunchy on their tongues. Roman tasted it, chewing thoughtfully. It was sweet, with a hint of chocolate and a bit of a crunch.

"Hmm... is this chocolate-covered pretzel?" Roman guessed.

Munch chuckled. "Very close, but not quite! It's a chocolate-covered rice puff."

The boys laughed, impressed by the surprising combination. Munch certainly had a talent for putting together snacks that tasted both familiar and unexpected.

"Alright, let's try the next one!" Jude said eagerly, ready for more.

Munch placed the next ingredient in their hands, and they both felt something soft and squishy. Roman bit into it and immediately recognized the familiar, gooey texture. "This one's a marshmallow! But... there's something extra in it."

Jude took another bite, concentrating on the flavour. "Is it... fruity?"

Munch clapped his hands. "Correct! It's a strawberry-flavoured marshmallow!"

The boys cheered, proud of their first successful guess. They were starting to get the hang of this mystery snack challenge.

"Ready for the next one?" Munch asked, his voice full of mischief.

They nodded eagerly, and Munch placed another treat in their mouths. This time, the flavour was salty and cheesy, with a satisfying crunch. Roman furrowed his brow, trying to place the taste.

"Hmm... it's crunchy like a chip, but it's got a cheesy flavour..." Roman murmured.

Jude snapped his fingers. "I know! It's a cheese cracker, but... it tastes like it's got some seasoning on it."

Munch chuckled. "Right again! It's a cheddar cheese cracker with garlic seasoning. You two have sharp taste buds!"

They shared a laugh, thrilled by the interesting combinations Munch had come up with. They'd never tried cheese crackers with garlic seasoning before, but they found they really liked it.

As the game went on, Munch continued to surprise them with unique flavours and textures. There was a dried pineapple piece dipped in caramel, a piece of popcorn coated in cinnamon sugar, and even a tiny yogurt-covered pretzel with a hint of lemon. Each snack was a fun challenge, keeping the boys guessing and giggling as they tried to identify each flavour.

Finally, Munch announced, "Alright, we're down to the last mystery ingredient. Are you ready for the grand finale?"

Roman and Jude nodded, excited to see what Munch had saved for last. Munch placed a final snack in their hands. It was crunchy on the outside, but as they bit into it, they tasted a surprising burst of sweetness.

"Whoa!" Jude said, chewing thoughtfully. "It's... sweet and fruity, but it's also crunchy. Is it a candy?"

Roman thought for a moment, savouring the flavour. "Is it... a dried berry dipped in chocolate?"

Munch let out a joyful laugh. "Close! It's a dried blueberry dipped in white chocolate."

The boys took off their blindfolds, grinning as they saw the delicious assortment of snacks in the bowl. It was a colorful, tasty mix of sweet, salty, and Savory treats, all uniquely combined to keep them guessing.

"That was so much fun, Munch!" Roman said, grabbing a handful of the snack mix and popping a few pieces into his mouth.

Jude nodded, still amazed by some of the surprising combinations. "Yeah, you really know how to make the best snacks. I never would have thought to put some of these flavours together!"

Munch beamed, his cheeks pink with pride. "I'm glad you liked it! Snack combinations are my specialty. Sometimes, the best treats are the ones you never expect."

To celebrate the end of the game, Munch handed each of them a small bag filled with their favorite mystery ingredients from the mix. "Here's a little snack mix for later. Consider it a prize for being such great snack detectives."

Roman and Jude thanked Munch, giving him a big hug. They couldn't wait to tell their parents about the fun challenge—and maybe even try to make their own mystery snack mixes sometime.

As they snacked and laughed together, they realized that Munch had turned an ordinary day into a memorable adventure, one filled with tasty surprises and a lot of laughter. And they knew that with Munch around, every snack was bound to be an exciting new discovery.

Chapter 30: The Secret Monster Message

One morning, Roman and Jude woke up to find something unusual on their pillows—a small, glittery envelope sealed with a shimmering wax stamp that had the outline of a tiny monster paw. They exchanged a look, their faces lighting up with excitement.

"What do you think it is?" Jude whispered, carefully picking up the envelope.

Roman examined it closely. "It looks like a secret message! From... the monsters?"

They opened the envelopes at the same time, and inside each one was a sparkling note written in curly, glowing letters. The letters seemed to shimmer and rearrange themselves, like they were alive with magic. Roman read the message aloud:

"Dear Roman and Jude,"

"You are invited on a secret adventure inside the house. Follow the clues to discover a surprise we've left just for you!"

Below the message was the first clue:

"Start where you wash and scrub, and find something hidden in a place you rub."

The boys looked at each other, their eyes wide with excitement. "The bathroom sink!" Roman guessed.

They raced to the bathroom, where they checked around the sink, peering under the soap dish and around the faucets. Finally, Jude spotted a small, glittery note tucked behind a bottle of hand soap. He grabbed it and read the next clue:

"Well done, explorers! For your next hint, look where the warmth helps clothes become mint."

Roman snapped his fingers. "The laundry room! It must be in the dryer!"

They hurried to the laundry room and opened the dryer door. Inside, they found another small envelope, this one dusted with tiny sparkles that puffed into the air as they opened it. Roman unfolded the note and read the next clue:

"Head to the place where you keep your feet snug. A little creature there gives a tug and a hug."

The boys exchanged confused looks for a moment before Jude's face lit up. "The shoe rack! It has to be!"

They ran to the entryway, where they kept their shoes. Sure enough, they found a little pouch tucked inside one of Jude's sneakers. Inside the pouch was another clue, written in Blinky's familiar glowing script:

"Almost there, keep up the fun! Head to the place where stories are spun."

Roman grinned. "The bookshelf! Let's go!"

They hurried to the living room, where their family kept their favorite storybooks. Roman scanned the shelves until he noticed a book that looked out of place—A Magical Guide to Monster Mischief, with sparkles glowing along its spine. He pulled it out, and a small envelope slipped out from between the pages.

Inside was the final clue:

"For the last stop, head to a place soft and wide, where friends gather for a joyful ride."

The boys immediately thought of the big, cozy couch in the living room. They dashed over, lifting the cushions and checking the space between them. At last, they found a tiny, glittery box nestled in the corner of the couch.

They carefully opened the box, and inside was a beautiful, sparkling charm shaped like a tiny star. The charm shimmered in rainbow colors, and it was attached to a small note:

"Congratulations, Roman and Jude! You've completed the secret monster adventure! This charm is a bit of magic from all of us. Keep it with you, and it will glow whenever you think of your monster friends. Love, Whiffle, Blinky, Munch, and Mumbles."

The boys grinned, holding up the charm together as it sparkled in the light. They couldn't wait to show it to their parents and tell them about the adventure.

"Best treasure hunt ever!" Jude declared.

Roman nodded, admiring the charm. "It's like having a piece of monster magic with us wherever we go."

The boys spent the rest of the day with their charm, laughing and talking about each clue, remembering the thrill of finding each glittery message hidden in unexpected places.

As the sun set, the charm gave off a warm glow, filling the room with a soft, magical light. And as they drifted off to sleep that night, Roman and Jude knew that their monster friends were never far away, ready to create more adventures and leave new surprises.

Chapter 31: Monster Graduation Day

It had been a long year filled with adventures, laughter, and unforgettable memories with their monster friends. Roman and Jude wanted to do something special to celebrate all the amazing times they'd shared, so they came up with a plan that would surprise their friends and show them just how much they meant to them—a Monster Graduation Day!

The boys got to work immediately, gathering supplies to create mini graduation caps and diplomas. They cut out small squares of cardboard for the caps, glued on tiny tassels made of yarn, and decorated the caps with glitter, of course. For the diplomas, they rolled up small pieces of paper tied with colorful ribbons, each one with a personal message for each monster.

On the day of the ceremony, Roman and Jude set up the living room with decorations and even a little podium made of pillows. They set out chairs for the monsters, filling the room with balloons and signs that read, "Congratulations, Graduates!" and "Class of Monster Magic!"

When everything was ready, the boys called out to their monster friends, who appeared with curious smiles, wondering what the surprise was about.

"Welcome, everyone!" Roman said, standing at the front like an official host. "Today is a very special day. We're here to celebrate all the fun, magical times we've shared with you."

Jude continued, holding up one of the mini caps. "And as a way to say thank you, we're going to have a Monster Graduation Ceremony!"

The monsters gasped with delight, their eyes widening as they saw the little caps and diplomas laid out for them. Whiffle clapped his hands, sprinkling a bit of glitter in the air as he giggled. "Oh, I've never graduated before! I feel so fancy!"

Munch, Blinky, and Mumbles all exchanged excited looks, clearly touched by the effort Roman and Jude had put into the ceremony.

The boys began calling each monster up to the pillow podium one by one, starting with Whiffle.

Graduate #1: Whiffle, the Glittery Monster

"Whiffle," Roman began with a smile, "you've brought so much sparkle and joy to our lives. You taught us how to find magic in the smallest things, and you've made every adventure more fun."

Jude placed the mini graduation cap on Whiffle's head, and Roman handed him a small diploma that read, "Whiffle—Master of Glitter and Giggles."

Whiffle took his diploma with a happy tear in his eye, thanking the boys as he made his way back to his seat, glitter trailing behind him.

Graduate #2: Munch, the Snack Monster

Next up was Munch. Jude grinned as he began, "Munch, you've filled our days with laughter, treats, and unforgettable snack creations. You've taught us that every adventure is better with a snack by your side."

Roman placed the cap on Munch's head, and Jude handed him a diploma that read, "Munch—Certified Snack Connoisseur and Master of Mystery Mixes."

Munch took a proud bite of a marshmallow he had hidden in his pouch, giving the boys a big hug before he sat back down, diploma in hand.

Graduate #3: Blinky, the Glow Monster

"Blinky," Roman said with a warm smile, "you've lit up our lives in ways we never imagined. You've shown us the beauty of light, even on the darkest days, and taught us how magical it can be."

Jude placed Blinky's cap on his head, and Roman handed him a diploma that read, "Blinky—Official Light Show Extraordinaire and Keeper of Glow."

Blinky's glow pulsed with joy, casting a soft, colorful light around the room. He bowed slightly, thanking them with a warm smile before he returned to his seat.

Graduate #4: Mumbles, the Misty Monster

Finally, it was Mumbles' turn. Jude spoke softly, "Mumbles, you've shown us the power of quiet magic. Your stories and soft mist have filled our lives with wonder, reminding us that sometimes the gentlest things are the most magical."

Roman placed the cap on Mumbles' head, and Jude handed him a diploma that read, "Mumbles—Master of Mist and Whisperer of Ghostly Giggles."

Mumbles' misty form shimmered, and he gave a humble nod, thanking the boys with a soft smile. He held his diploma close, clearly touched by the gesture.

The Graduation Speech and Celebration

After all the monsters had received their diplomas, Roman and Jude gathered them together for a "class photo," taking a picture of their monster friends all wearing their mini graduation caps, diplomas in hand. The monsters posed proudly, laughing and waving at the camera, their faces glowing with happiness.

Then, Jude gave a little graduation speech. "Thank you, all of you, for being the best friends we could ever ask for. You've made every day an adventure, and we're so lucky to have shared these moments with you."

The monsters cheered, clapping their hands and sprinkling the air with glitter and mist. Whiffle even tossed a bit of sparkle confetti, which drifted through the air like shimmering stars.

To end the ceremony, Munch brought out a "graduation snack buffet" he had prepared, complete with glittery popcorn, mini cupcakes, and marshmallows shaped like graduation caps. The boys and monsters shared a feast, laughing and reminiscing about their favorite moments together.

Blinky turned down the lights, creating a soft glow that made the room feel cozy and magical. They all gathered around, snuggling under blankets and pillows, telling stories and sharing jokes. Each monster took turns recalling a funny or touching memory from the past year, filling the room with warmth and laughter.

As the evening wound down, Whiffle stood up and raised his sparkly cap. "Here's to more adventures, more giggles, and more magic—together!"

The boys and monsters all cheered, lifting their snacks in a toast to friendship and the magical memories they'd shared.

It was a perfect end to a perfect day, and as Roman and Jude headed to bed that night, they felt a warmth in their hearts, knowing they'd created a celebration that their monster friends would remember forever.

The Monster Graduation Day had been a beautiful tribute to friendship, laughter, and the magic they'd created together, a memory that would sparkle in their hearts for years to come.

Chapter 32: The Nighttime Glitter Hunt

It was a clear, starry night, and Roman and Jude were just about to head to bed when Whiffle appeared at their bedroom window, his face beaming with excitement. He seemed to sparkle even more than usual, his eyes twinkling with a hint of mystery.

"Psst! Boys!" Whiffle whispered, waving them over. "Would you like to go on a Nighttime Glitter Hunt with me?"

Roman and Jude's eyes lit up, and they immediately scrambled out of bed, pulling on their shoes and jackets. "What's a glitter hunt?" Jude asked, his voice filled with excitement.

Whiffle grinned, sprinkling a handful of glitter in the air. "It's a nighttime adventure where we search for rare, sparkling treasures hidden around the yard. The starlight and moonlight help reveal these hidden gems, and only those with a sense of adventure—and a sprinkle of magic—can find them."

The boys couldn't resist. They grabbed their flashlights, though Whiffle promised that they might not need them, and followed him out to the backyard, where the night was calm and the stars twinkled brightly overhead.

The First Sparkle: The Stardust Shell

As they entered the backyard, Whiffle led them to the flower bed near the fence. "Our first treasure is something small but very special. Look closely near the flowers, and let the moonlight guide you."

Roman and Jude crouched down, letting their eyes adjust to the moonlight. Suddenly, Jude spotted something glimmering in the soil—a small, iridescent shell that seemed to be dusted with tiny, twinkling specks.

"I found something!" Jude said, carefully picking up the shell. It glowed faintly, as if it held a tiny piece of the stars themselves.

"That's a Stardust Shell," Whiffle explained softly. "They're left behind by gentle night creatures and absorb starlight to shimmer just like the sky. You're lucky to find one!"

The boys admired the shell, captivated by its soft glow, before tucking it safely into Jude's pocket for safekeeping.

The Second Sparkle: The Moonbeam Feather

Whiffle then led them to a tree near the back of the yard, where a low-hanging branch cast soft shadows on the ground. "Now, we're looking for something that catches the moonbeam's glow. It might be closer to the ground, near the roots."

Roman knelt down, carefully moving leaves aside, when he saw a delicate feather lying on the grass. Unlike any feather he'd seen, it seemed to glow with a silver light, reflecting the moon's rays.

"Is this it?" Roman asked, holding the feather up to Whiffle.

Whiffle's eyes sparkled with pride. "That's a Moonbeam Feather. It's rare and special, left by mystical birds that only fly under the moonlight. They say moonbeam feathers bring sweet dreams and good luck."

Roman carefully placed the feather in his pocket, feeling like he'd discovered a real treasure.

The Third Sparkle: The Glow Stone

As they moved toward the garden path, Whiffle stopped and pointed to the ground near a cluster of small rocks. "Somewhere here is a stone that glows with its own light. It's not just any stone; it's a Glow Stone."

The boys scanned the ground, their eyes searching for a sign of light. After a few moments, they noticed a faint glow coming from between two larger rocks.

"There it is!" Jude exclaimed, reaching down to pick it up. The stone was small, smooth, and had a soft blue glow, pulsing gently in his hand.

Whiffle nodded approvingly. "Glow Stones have a bit of natural magic. They help guide anyone who feels lost, even in the darkest places."

Roman held the stone with a look of awe. "We'll always have a bit of light with this."

Whiffle smiled, clearly pleased. "Exactly. It's a treasure for those who seek light, even in the night."

The Final Sparkle: The Star Flower Petal

For the last treasure, Whiffle led them to a quiet corner of the yard where a small patch of flowers grew, their petals closed for the night. "Look closely," he whispered. "A Star Flower might be hiding here, waiting to be found."

Roman and Jude knelt down, searching the plants. Suddenly, they spotted a single, tiny petal lying on the grass. Unlike the other flowers, this petal had a shimmer to it, as though it held the light of a thousand stars.

Jude picked it up gently, his face filled with wonder. "It's beautiful," he murmured, holding the petal up to the moonlight, where it sparkled softly.

"That's a Star Flower Petal," Whiffle explained. "They only bloom at night, and their petals are said to hold wishes. Keep it safe, and it may just help a wish come true."

Roman and Jude carefully tucked the petal into Jude's pocket, their hearts full of excitement at having found such a rare and magical treasure.

The Night's End: A Magical Reflection

As they gathered their treasures, Whiffle led them to the middle of the yard, where they could see the stars sparkling brightly above. They held their finds—the stardust shell, the moonbeam feather, the glow stone, and the star flower petal—and admired the faint glows and sparkles they emitted.

"Thank you for taking us on this glitter hunt, Whiffle," Roman said, his voice filled with gratitude.

Whiffle nodded, his eyes twinkling. "Magic is everywhere, boys. Sometimes it's hidden, sometimes it's right in front of you, but it's always there if you look with wonder."

The boys sat with Whiffle under the starlit sky, feeling grateful for the magical treasures and the special night they'd shared.

When they returned inside, Roman and Jude carefully arranged their treasures on their nightstand, feeling as if they'd brought a piece of the night's magic indoors with them. The glow of the treasures filled their room with a gentle light, a reminder of the nighttime glitter hunt and the wonders they'd found together.

As they drifted off to sleep, they felt like they were still under the stars, surrounded by the soft glow of their magical finds. And they knew that no matter how ordinary a day or night might seem, with Whiffle and their monster friends, even the simplest adventures could become extraordinary.

Chapter 33: Sammy Joins the Fun

One bright morning, Roman and Jude were in the backyard with Whiffle, Munch, Blinky, and Mumbles, planning their next big adventure. They were so wrapped up in their excitement that they didn't hear the footsteps behind them—until a familiar voice called out.

"So, what kind of mischief are you all getting into today?" their dad, Sammy, asked with a warm smile.

The boys turned around, surprised and thrilled. "Dad! You want to join us?" Roman asked, his face lighting up with excitement.

Sammy grinned, a twinkle in his eye. "I think it's about time I joined one of these adventures. I've missed a lot of monster fun over the years, and it's time to catch up!"

Whiffle clapped his hands with joy, leaving a little burst of glitter in the air. "Sammy! It's been far too long! We're thrilled to have you back with us!"

The monsters gathered around, giving Sammy little hugs and excited cheers. Munch offered him a snack, Blinky brightened his glow, and Mumbles floated around, adding a misty sparkle to the scene. They were just as excited as the boys to have their old friend back.

A Trip Down Memory Lane

Before they began their adventure, the monsters wanted to revisit a few old memories with Sammy. They brought out a few keepsakes from their past: a tiny, sparkly shell Whiffle had saved from one of their glitter hunts, a feather from an old pillow fort pillow, and even a few crumbs from one of Munch's legendary snack mixes.

"Remember the midnight glitter hunt?" Whiffle asked, holding up the shell.

Sammy chuckled. "Oh, I remember! You taught me how to find hidden treasures in the dark. I'd forgotten how magical that night felt."

Blinky floated over, his glow warming as he recalled their times together. "And all those light shows in the rain! Remember when we turned the puddles into little pools of color?"

Sammy nodded, his face full of nostalgia. "I'd never seen rain look so beautiful. You all brought so much wonder into those simple moments."

Roman and Jude listened in awe, loving the stories of their dad's monster-filled adventures. They couldn't wait to show Sammy some of the new activities they'd come up with!

A New Adventure: The Glittery Scavenger Hunt

To celebrate Sammy joining the fun, Roman and Jude decided to create a special scavenger hunt with a mix of old and new surprises. They placed glittery clues all over the yard, each one leading to a small memory or a new activity that combined their adventures with the monsters and Sammy's past ones.

The first clue led them to the flower bed, where they found a small note tucked behind a bush. "Return to where we once found our glow stones," it read.

Sammy laughed, recalling the spot near the flower bed where he and Blinky had once found glowing stones. When they arrived, Blinky placed a new glow stone in Sammy's hand. "One for old times' sake," he said with a wink.

The next clue led them to the big oak tree where they'd had countless picnic adventures. Munch had left a small, sparkly snack mix there, a combination of some of Sammy's favorite treats along with a few new additions the boys loved.

Sammy took a bite, savouring the mix of flavours. "I think you've outdone yourself, Munch," he said, chuckling as Munch puffed up with pride.

The Ultimate Pillow Fort

The final stop on the scavenger hunt was in the living room, where they had set up the biggest, comfiest pillow fort ever. Whiffle had added his famous glittery pillows, Blinky created a soft glow inside, and Mumbles added a light mist, making the whole fort feel like a dream.

Sammy crawled inside with the boys, laughing as they snuggled into the fluffy pillows. "This is even better than the forts we made back in the day," Sammy said, marveling at the cozy hideaway.

Inside the fort, the monsters took turns sharing their favorite memories with Sammy, while the boys added a few of their own. They laughed about the glitter mishaps, the monster snack experiments, and even the times they'd all gotten "lost" in their imaginations.

A Special Gift from the Monsters

As the day wound down, the monsters gathered together to give Sammy a small but meaningful gift. Whiffle handed him a charm made from pieces of their adventures—a glow stone from Blinky, a tiny glitter shell from Whiffle, a snack charm from Munch, and a misty feather from Mumbles. The charm sparkled with every color, a symbol of all the fun and magic they'd shared.

"Sammy," Whiffle said, "we wanted you to have this as a reminder that no matter where life takes you, the magic of our friendship is always with you."

Sammy took the charm, his eyes misty with gratitude. "Thank you, my friends. This means more than you know."

Roman and Jude watched, feeling proud to see how much their dad's friendship with the monsters meant to everyone. They hugged Sammy, knowing that they'd keep making magical memories together for years to come.

The Night Ends with Laughter and Light

As the evening settled in, Blinky created one last light show in the backyard. The raindrops from a light drizzle sparkled with his glow, creating a soft, colorful display. They all sat together, laughing, reminiscing, and enjoying the beautiful moment.

When it was time to say goodnight, the monsters promised Sammy they'd always be there, ready for more fun anytime he wanted. And as

Sammy tucked Roman and Jude into bed that night, he knew that the magic of friendship, family, and imagination would keep bringing them together, creating new memories with every adventure.

With his heart full of joy, Sammy placed the charm on the boys' nightstand, a glowing reminder of all the magical moments they'd shared with their monster friends. And as they drifted off to sleep, the boys knew they were part of something truly special—a bond of love, laughter, and endless adventures with their dad and their magical monster family.

Chapter 34: The Time Capsule

One afternoon, as Roman and Jude were playing in the backyard with their monster friends, they came up with a unique idea.

"What if we made a time capsule?" Roman suggested, his eyes sparkling with excitement. "We could fill it with keepsakes from all our adventures with the monsters, so we never forget these moments!"

Whiffle, Munch, Blinky, and Mumbles all perked up at the idea, their faces lighting up with excitement.

"A time capsule?" Whiffle repeated, twirling in the air and sprinkling glitter around. "That sounds magical! And we could dig it up one day to remember everything."

With everyone on board, they quickly gathered supplies—a small, sturdy box, and lots of tiny bags and pouches to keep each item safe. They decided they'd each pick something special from their adventures, something that held a memory they cherished.

Gathering Keepsakes

The first to add something was Whiffle. He fluttered around the backyard, looking for the perfect item. Finally, he pulled a tiny vial of glitter from his bag, holding it up proudly.

"This is my Friendship Glitter," Whiffle explained. "It's a mix of all the glitter I've used during our best adventures. Every time you open it, it will remind you of the magic and fun we had together."

Roman carefully placed the vial in the box, feeling a rush of warmth knowing that a piece of Whiffle's magic would always be preserved.

Next, Munch rummaged through his snack pouch, looking for something extra special. With a big grin, he pulled out a miniature bag of his "Mystery Snack Mix" and placed it in the box.

"This mix has a bit of everything—sweet, salty, crunchy, and even a surprise or two!" Munch explained. "It's a little reminder that sometimes, life's best moments are the unexpected ones."

Jude placed the bag in the capsule, chuckling at the thought of one day finding Munch's mystery mix and remembering all the funny snack challenges they'd had.

Blinky floated over next, his glow softening as he pulled a small, smooth glow stone from his pouch. "This glow stone holds a bit of my light," he said, smiling. "Whenever you see it, you'll remember that even in the darkest times, a little light can make everything brighter."

Roman took the glow stone, feeling its soft warmth, and gently set it in the box.

Finally, Mumbles floated forward with a misty feather. "This feather is from our nighttime adventures," he whispered. "It's filled with ghostly giggles and memories of all the times we laughed together under the stars."

The boys carefully placed Mumbles' feather in the capsule, feeling like they were capturing the very spirit of their friendship.

Adding Personal Keepsakes

Roman and Jude thought about what they could add to the time capsule that would remind them of these amazing times. After some thought, Roman chose a small drawing he'd made of the monster family on one of their first adventures together. He carefully folded it and placed it in the box.

Jude added a small notebook where he'd jotted down funny sayings from each monster, along with his favorite memories. "This way, when we open the capsule, we'll have a journal of all the silly things we've done together."

The monsters gathered around, admiring the keepsakes, each item carrying a piece of their adventures, laughter, and love.

Burying the Time Capsule

With everything in place, they closed the box, tying it with a bright, sparkly ribbon that Whiffle had brought. Together, they found a special spot under the big oak tree in the backyard, where they'd had many picnics and games.

Munch handed each of them a small shovel, and they took turns digging a spot deep enough to keep the time capsule safe. Once the hole was ready, they placed the box inside, each one touching it one last time, feeling the importance of the moment.

"Now, we bury it," Blinky said, his glow warming as he looked at each of his friends. "And one day, when we open it, we'll relive every single adventure."

The boys and monsters took turns covering the box with soil, patting it down gently. When they were finished, Whiffle sprinkled a bit of glitter on top, creating a sparkling mark that would remind them of the capsule's location.

Making a Promise

They all sat around the buried capsule, feeling the significance of what they'd done. Whiffle placed a gentle hand on Roman's shoulder, his eyes bright with emotion.

"No matter how many years go by, or how far we go, we'll always have these memories," he said softly. "This time capsule is a piece of our friendship, preserved forever."

The boys hugged each monster, feeling grateful for the moments they'd shared and the adventures that had brought them closer together. "We promise to come back and open it one day, all together," Jude said, a warm smile on his face.

As the sun began to set, casting a golden glow over the yard, they sat in a circle, their hands linked. Blinky glowed softly, and Mumbles' mist created a gentle, magical haze around them. For a moment, it felt like they were the only ones in the world, wrapped in the warmth of friendship.

With a final smile, they whispered their promise to the buried capsule, a vow to keep their memories close, even as they grew older.

As they headed inside, each of them felt the magic of the moment lingering, knowing that they'd created something special, something that would connect them forever. And though it was buried deep in the earth, the memories in that time capsule sparkled as brightly as the stars above.

Disclaimer

This book is a work of fiction meant to entertain and inspire young readers with tales of imagination, friendship, and a little bit of magical fun. All characters, events, and magical creatures within are entirely fictional, and any resemblance to real people, places, or events is purely coincidental.

Parents, please note that while the story includes playful adventures with imaginary monsters, it is intended to foster creativity, joy, and a sense of wonder. No real monsters were involved in the making of this book (though we wish they had been!).

Enjoy this story with an open heart, a love for adventure, and perhaps a snack or two—just in case any silly, snack-loving monsters happen to be nearby!